Breathing Wisteria

Finding Forever Book 4

USA TODAY BESTSELLING AUTHOR

AMALI ROSE

Breathing Wisteria
Copyright © 2019 by Amali Rose

This book is a work of fiction. Names and characters, places, and incidents are the product of the author's imagination or are used fictitiously. Any resemblance to actual events, locales, or persons, living or dead, is coincidental.

Editing: Ellie McLove - My Brother's Editor
Proofreading: Judy Zweifel - Judy's Proofreading
Cover Design: Ben Ellis – Tall Story Designs
Cover Image: Adobestock

Breathing Wisteria

Finding Forever Book 4

USA TODAY BESTSELLING AUTHOR
AMALI ROSE

This book is for Kim.
For chasing your dreams and fighting for your HEA.
You inspire me.

"Dare to live the life you have dreamed for yourself. Go forward and make your dreams come true."
Ralph Waldo Emerson

Synopsis

Once bitten, twice shy. These days, true love can kiss her ass.

Finding your soulmate at a young age is supposed to set you up for a lifetime of happiness. But in Wyatt Monroe's case, it taught her that forever love and soulmates are nothing but a great big pile of junk—a bedtime story not found in reality.

Ten years ago, she lost everything she truly cared about. Now, she's guarding her heart fiercely, more than content with her solitary existence as an artist in New York.

She doesn't want the fairytale.
She doesn't want a knight in shining armor.
She's more than capable of saving herself, thank you very much.

That is, until Flynn Maguire tracks her down. He's tired of hiding in his music from what they were. A decade of running from his feelings is far too long and now he's determined to reclaim the life that should have been his.

But determination will only get you so far, and when the glare of public scrutiny shines an unkind light on their troubled past, they need to choose—

Let their past hurt tear them apart yet again, or stand together and learn that true love really does conquer all...

PROLOGUE

WYATT

*T*en Years Earlier

Smoke.

My nostrils twitch as the subtle acrid smell hits them and a sliver of unease curls itself around my consciousness.

The club is crowded, and I'm jostled carelessly between a sea of sweaty bodies. My hand instinctively finds my belly and I internally curse Flynn for convincing me to come tonight.

I crane my neck, searching for the source of the putrid smell, but I can barely see past the people surrounding me. Their clammy skin pressing against my own combined with their loud voices ringing in my ear, the atmosphere practically suffocates me.

My breathing begins to quicken. Short, shallow breaths that I have to fight to get into my lungs, heighten my anxiety and the mild apprehension I was feeling morphs quickly into full-blown dread that thrashes violently through my veins.

Closing my eyes, I try to block out the crowd around me and concentrate on Flynn's voice, which floats above the cheers and catcalls. My vision is blocked from my position over here, along the side of the room where I, wrongly, assumed I could avoid the crush of the congested dance floor.

That's when it happens.

With my eyes squeezed shut, one hand pressed against my hammering chest and the other curled protectively over my stomach. My brain shuts down, focusing only on the voice of the man I love, singing the song he wrote about us. About cherry Chapstick and cheap beer.

The moment my life was forever changed.

One word screamed.

Hundreds of bodies pushing, fighting each other, chased by the cruel heat and wicked burn.

I'm shoved forcefully up against the wall as people lose all sense of decency in their own fight for safety. My eyes flicker to my left and I see the orange flames dancing with the plumes of black smoke above the stage. My heart sinks and I unconsciously begin fighting against the crowd. Sweat prickles along every inch of my skin and I fight every instinct in me as I try to make my way toward Flynn.

A tall guy stops right in front of me, his face is panicked, and I can see a fear in his eyes that I know is echoed in my own. He bends down and grabs my shoulders, his fingertips digging in painfully. "Go the other way!" he screams in my face, his spit coating me. Shaking my head, I push past him and hear him mutter, "Stupid bitch."

The pungent smoke has filled the room and as my lungs struggle to cope, screaming for fresh air, I become disoriented. I spin around, my eyes burning while I attempt to gather my wits. But when a stray elbow connects with my already aching temple, I lose my balance, falling to the ground. And in a moment that I know will forever be imprinted on me, amidst the cacophony of terrified screams, flailing bodies, and heart-wrenching terror, I lose everything that I love.

CHAPTER ONE

WYATT

This room is full of love. It's almost a tangible entity that I can physically feel and a small smile dances across my lips as I stand in a corner, taking it all in. My smile explodes into a loud laugh as I watch one of my best friends, Cassidy, chase her three-year-old twins around the room, a small plate of food in each hand and long cotton-candy-pink hair streaming behind her.

"I don't know how she handles those two." A gentle voice has me turning, and I see the last member of our trio, Skye, standing to my right, her own full mouth tilted in an amused smile.

"I struggle with my two, and Poppy is barely even walking. If I were getting double-teamed like that, I'd be waving the white flag." She groans.

I bring the champagne glass left over from our earlier toasts to my mouth and take a small sip, enjoying the way the bubbles tickle my throat on their way down.

"You know what?" My eyebrow quirks as I observe my beautifully ridiculous friend, who is the perfect, contradictory mix of virtue and venom, with her children. "If I ever doubted the existence of karma, that doubt vanished when she had Mack and Seb. I mean, look at that." I raise a finger from my glass and point toward Cassidy's parents on the opposite side of the room. They're watching the quiet chaos their grandchildren are causing, gleefully. "Cass' mom is practically giddy watching her chase those babies around. I'd say that's a pretty blatant example of karma biting you on the ass."

Skye snorts out an adorable laugh as she takes in the Jensens' expressions before she turns her attention to the newly engaged couple slow dancing in the middle of the room. The reason we're here celebrating tonight.

"So, how long do you think until those two start popping out some beautiful babies?" Skye tilts her head to Ethan and Layla, her warm blue eyes softening as we watch Ethan's grip on his new fiancée tighten and he pulls her even closer.

The pain that rips through my chest at her question is visceral and it takes everything I have to keep myself upright and a smile plastered on my face.

"My guess is we get an announcement in the next six months. I can't see them waiting," I reply, confidently.

Skye continues to watch them contemplatively, and I allow my mind to wander. My thoughts are trailing into dangerous territory when her next words take me completely by surprise and quickly snap me out of my dark reminiscences.

"I guess it's just you that we have to worry about now."

I whip my head around to face her, my eyes wide in surprise.

"What?"

She reaches across and takes the glass from my hand before gulping down the remains and placing the empty glass on a table beside her.

"Well, it's just you now. The rest of us are all married off, or as good as. Babies are popping out all over the place." She looks pointedly over to a large table where Cassidy has managed to wrangle Mackenzie and Sebastian, getting them seated alongside Skye's children, Summer and Poppy. Cassidy and her husband, Mason, are looking flustered as they deal with a pissed-off Mack (seriously, can you say, like mother, like daughter?) and Skye's husband, Ben, feeds Poppy and watches on indulgently while Seb sneaks his much-loved potato chips to his much-loved Summer.

"Now we just need to get you married off and we can all be horrible hot messes together!"

My face heats at her declaration and for the millionth time since I met these women all those years ago, I regret holding on to my secrets so fiercely.

"Yeah, that's not going to happen, sweetie, so don't hold your breath." I hate the steel tone my voice carries.

Skye's eyes narrow shrewdly as she watches me and I'm sure she must be able to hear my heart thrashing wildly in my chest. Unbidden, my hand flies to my breast, my palm attempting to soothe the pain away.

"One day you're going to tell me, you know."

The ache intensifies at her words and a flush of anxiety washes over me.

"Tell you what?" Denial. I'm an old hand at this particular method of self-preservation and the words slip out of my mouth with practiced ease.

Skye's hand finds mine and she gives me a gentle squeeze.

"When you're ready, I will be here for you. I need you to know that."

One thing you learn about Skye very quickly is that she may look like an angel, all innocent beauty and wide-eyed optimism, but she will have your back, no questions asked. Anytime, anywhere.

I clench my jaw and my teeth grind against each other. A lump solidifies in my throat making it impossible for me to do anything other than nod.

No matter how desperately I wish I could unburden my heart, it's impossible to change the past. I have no choice but to continue to keep these scars hidden because, honestly, I'm not sure they could ever forgive me for concealing such a huge piece of my heart from them.

As if this moment couldn't get any worse, the song that was the soundtrack to the worst year of my life starts playing over the sound system. A song declaring true love and the desire to save something worth fighting for. Memories immediately run through my mind as I relive it all. Long fingers scrawling words, madly trying to get down the thoughts, emotions, and fears before they disappeared forever.

Skye's reaction to the song is vastly different. Her face transforms when she hears the opening chords, the air between us immediately defusing, and her hand grips my wrist.

"Oh my God, I love this song! Can you watch the girls for a minute?" She gives me her best puppy dog eyes. "I want to dance with Ben."

Slipping on my best neutral mask, I agree and follow her back to our table.

"C'mon, babycakes, hand the mac and cheese to Wyatt and come and dance with me."

Ben grins beautifully at his wife, his eyes crinkling up in amusement, and my mask slips briefly as I let a moment of wistfulness overwhelm me.

Remembering, just for a brief moment, the way guarded brown eyes used to look at me as though I was perfection personified.

Until they didn't.

Shaking my head slightly, I reach over and take the small bowl from his hands and gesture for Ben to go. He leans over and places a swift kiss on my cheek, along with a whispered thank-you.

I can't stop my eyes from following them across the dance floor and just when I start to feel those old papered-over cracks in my heart start to split again, Cassidy's voice snaps me out of my reverie.

"Ugh, those two make me want to puke. No one should still be that lovey-dovey after all this time. That is not what marriage is."

Mason smirks across at her, running a hand through his tousled brown hair. "I don't know, we were pretty lovey-dovey this morning, if you recall."

She narrows her eyes at him, and I prepare myself for whatever scathing comment is to come. Looking at Mason, his grin has widened and he's practically vibrating with anticipation. I suppress an eye roll. I've never met a man who enjoys getting his balls busted so much by his wife.

But before she can say anything, a loud cry sounds when Mackenzie falls off her chair, crashing to the ground. Cassidy rushes to pick her up and is soothing her when Seb abruptly stands up on his chair, looking anxiously around the room. Mason tells him to sit down in a commanding voice that almost has my ass finding a seat, but Seb just looks at him, his eyes wide.

"I need to go to the potty, Daddy."

Mason moves quickly, reaching over to pick him up, but when his hand lands on Seb's butt a loud groan escapes.

"You didn't make it, huh, bud?"

Cassidy continues soothing Mackenzie, who is still loudly screaming and looks at her husband and son, both of whom are now covered in pee.

She turns to me slowly, a sardonic look on her face.

"This," she says calmly. "This is marriage."

The bed dips beneath me and I flop back onto the mattress, arms spread, eyes closed.

Tonight was… I'm not even sure what it was.

Seeing my friends all together in one place, so happy with their partners and children, it created a huge mess of conflicting emotions.

And memories. So many painful memories.

Sheets rustle under me when I turn to my side and reach under the bed for the box. The box.

Where said memories are supposed to go and die a swift death.

But they don't. They merely hibernate in there until the next time my defenses are down, and I can't stop from torturing myself.

Sitting back up, I cross my legs and place the large box over my legs.

Five years. Inside this ridiculous-looking box covered in garish pink flamingos is five years of my life.

Four years of immeasurable joy. One year of immeasurable pain.

My throat tightens while my fingertips move, almost involuntarily, ghosting across the top and my heart thunders as I try to compose myself before facing my nightmare.

So, essentially, my usual reaction.

Taking a deep breath, I do my best to steady my hands and I slowly remove the lid. Lying on top is the framed photograph that sat on my bedside table for almost two years. I'm wearing a gorgeous pink dress with a long, ruffled skirt. If I close my eyes, I can still feel the soft material tickling my ankles.

I tripped over that damn thing so many times and

very nearly ended the night with a sprained ankle. Plus, it clashed wildly with my bright red hair, but I couldn't have cared less. I loved that dress so damn much and the boy staring down at me in the photograph seemed to agree.

Although, if I recall he was just as eager to get it off me as he was to admire it on.

I reach up and scrub a hand over my nose which is developing the unmistakable tingle of oncoming tears. Christ, I must be getting sappy in my old age, I normally last longer than this.

Sliding my eyes back to the photo, I take in the tall, built guy next to me, his intense brown eyes glued to me as I grin at the camera. Full lips that so rarely lifted into anything more than a dirty smirk, are curled up into a smile so big, it almost rivals my own.

He towers over me, and I remember the sense of safety that used to overwhelm me every time his arm slid around my shoulders and he would pull me in, close to his body. The sensation of his calloused fingers on my skin when they would inevitably start teasing along the curve of my neck.

He was my home. Wherever he was, that was where I was supposed to be.

Where I wanted to be.

Until I didn't.

Sighing, I shove the picture back into the box, aggressively.

Flynn. Fucking. Maguire.

One of the biggest singer-songwriters in the music

industry is my ex. My first love. The man I stupidly thought I would spend the rest of my life with.

Now, as the song says, he's just somebody I used to know. Somebody who is impossible to escape, no matter how hard I try. His face appears on my Facebook feed incessantly, in magazines, on television.

Don't even get me started on his music. It's everywhere. So many songs that he wrote when we were together, and I'm immediately propelled back in time, remembering the way his voice would deepen when he had an idea that he was passionate about. The way he would get so lost in creating he would forget to do simple things, like, you know, eat.

Biting down hard on my lip, I dive back in, sorting my way through piles of random snapshots, corny love notes and lyrics scrawled in his god-awful writing.

The pain of missing him is savage, intensifying as each memory washes over me, and only when I notice the wet heat on my face, do I realize that my tears have finally fallen.

I allow myself to feel this so rarely and this is exactly why. It's too much. Too much pain, too much regret.

Too much everything.

I begin to gently place everything back in the box when my eye catches on the corner of a picture sticking out of an envelope. Suddenly I miss the pain of only moments before, because this agony right here? It is the soul-crushing, life-altering kind.

Pain that changes you into a person you no longer recognize.

Dropping everything in my hands, I pull the photo out of the yellowing envelope and lock onto the grainy black and white picture.

My chest heaves, my eyes burn, and my throat feels as though it's closing up as that tiny image reduces me to a violent vortex of grief.

Quickly stuffing the photo back into the box, I dump everything else on top of it and replace the lid, wishing desperately it was that easy to hide my pain away. I lean down and shove the evidence of my life gone so wrong under the bed, before giving in to the cleansing sobs that are fighting to escape.

Reaching over to my purse that is still lying on the bed, I pull out my cell phone and manage to calm myself so I'm only a snotty, hiccupping mess, rather than a snotty, sobbing one.

Unlocking my screen, I search through my contacts and pull up the name I should have called a long time ago.

With a shaking finger I press the call button, take a deep breath, and wait for the call to connect.

"Fuck." The word escapes my mouth with a hiss as her mouth slides up and down my shaft. Warm and wet, and completely fucking perfect.

The sound of her gagging grabs my attention and I realize I've broken her golden BJ rule. No deep throating.

Pulling back, that luscious mouth releases me and I'm left with just her tiny hand grasping me, slowly jerking me off.

Too slowly to get me off, and she fucking knows it. Bright green eyes gaze up and I feel my dick jerk in her hand.

"I've warned you about that, Irish," she reprimands. I try to hide my smirk because, seriously? Only this woman could scold me during a blow job and still have me painfully hard.

"Lost my head for a second." I thread my hand through her long, auburn hair and electricity pulses through me as I drag her up to stand. "Both of them."

"Jesus, that was lame."

I open my mouth to defend myself but, luckily for me, this girl has a different, much better, use for my mouth and I wrap my arms around her, enjoying the slide of her tongue against mine. The gentle nips at my bottom lip that have me rocking against her, trying to create the friction we both need. Her noises are becoming more and more desperate and, forgetting any pretense of gentleness, I roughly pick her up, determined not to wait a second longer to be buried balls deep in her sweet pussy.

She wraps her legs around me, and it may have been a while since we were last here, but our bodies haven't forgotten exactly how good we can make each other feel.

I pull her even closer and I can feel exactly how wet she is as she grinds against my bare skin. Sliding my hand down, I cup her ass and the moan that falls from my lips is so loud it practically echoes around the hotel room.

Reaching around from behind, I move her panties to the side and, with no preamble at all, push my middle finger inside her. Her responding gasp brings a smirk to my lips. I fucking love every one of her filthy sounds.

Her head falls to my chest, a halo of red surrounding her face and she pushes back against my finger.

"More," she rasps.

Happy to oblige, I fill her with a second finger, reveling in her breathless whimpers. Stopping my movement toward the bed, I abruptly spin her around, push her up against the wall, and slam my mouth to hers. She opens for me immediately and the taste of her, combined with the feel of her pussy tightening around my fingers, has me desperate to come.

Just as I am sliding a third finger in, the irritating buzz of my cell phone starts up, distracting us both.

"Ignore it." I sound like a commanding asshole, but if I don't get her off in the next thirty seconds, my head will explode.

And, again, I mean both of them.

She takes me at my word, and I close my eyes when her hands begin teasing down my chest, nails applying just enough pressure. She's close to my cock, so fucking close, when the phone starts back up.

Her movements still and she looks up at me, her eyes sad, reminding me of the last time we saw each other.

"You should get that, it's probably important."

"No." My voice is firm. "This is more important."

"This isn't real, Flynn. You know that." A gentle kiss is placed on my mouth. "Answer the phone, baby."

I wake with a start, my phone jumping all over the side table, blaring the annoying tone I use in an effort to force myself to answer calls.

Still half-awake and pissed as all fuck to have been woken from my dream, I snatch the cell up without looking at the caller ID.

"What." Too annoyed for niceties, my tone is harsh.

"Well, good morning to you too, grump."

Charlie's gentle voice has me on alert straight away.

"What's wrong? Is she okay?" I try to tamp down my apprehension, but it's hopeless. Wyatt Monroe will always be my Achilles heel and I have no fucking problem with that.

"Relax, cowboy." A small smile crosses my lips at the old nickname. "She's..." Her voice trails off and the familiar anxiety-driven numbness settles over me.

"She's what, Charlie. Tell me."

"She's not doing great, okay?" Her voice is reluctant, and I know she'll be beating herself up for this phone call, worried that she's betraying her friend. Charlie has been Wyatt's best friend since they were eight years old when they bonded over their love of Reese's Pieces and Nick Carter.

Hell, she was one of my best friends for a few years. Before everything happened. Now, not so much.

Luckily for me, she's a stand-up person and stays in touch, albeit rarely and irregularly, to keep me updated on how Wyatt's going.

"I think— no, I know, she's struggling at the moment. Her friends are all getting married and having babies." Her voice cracks on the last word and I feel that crack resonate in me. Just as broken as I am.

"Anyway, she's been doing it tough for a while now, I guess, but you know her." A somber chuckle carries over the line. "She just buries her head in the sand and pretends that everything is okay."

It takes everything I have in me not to let my bitterness rain down at that giant understatement.

"I guess you know that better than anyone, though."

"Yeah," I answer, my voice brusque. "But she called you and talked it out? She's good?"

My questions are met with a silence that makes every one of my pulse points roar to life. We've never had this conversation without it ending in one fact. Wyatt is okay.

Because as long as she's okay, I can breathe.

"I think…" Again, her voice trails off and the combination of frustration from my earlier dream and annoyance at this beating-around-the-bush bullshit causes me to snap.

"For Christ's sake, stop with the fucking dramatics and just tell me."

"Calm down, Flynn. This isn't easy for me, you know." Her voice thickens as though talking is difficult, and if I was a better man, I would regret the way I spoke to her.

If I was a better man.

"Charlie…"

"Okay, okay. Jesus." She inhales deeply before letting out a nerve-riddled sigh. "I think you need to go and see her. You two need to sort your shit out. I have no idea what that looks like, or what it involves, but she deserves to have some peace and she's never going to get it the way you guys left things." A pause. "Neither of you will."

My fingers tighten around the phone and a persistent throb starts beating in my temple. I have a performance on *The Graham Norton Show* tonight and then the European leg of this shitty promotional tour is done. I have a week before I have to start it all over again back in the States. The perfect opportunity to go off the grid.

Memories start to play on a loop through my mind and my heart picks up speed at the thought of seeing her. Touching her. Smelling her.

And, there it is. The creeper-line. I try to rein myself back in.

"I think this would be good for both of you," Charlie's voice interrupts. "You need to give her a chance to say the things she never got to." Her voice remains neutral, but I feel the accusation like a right hook and just like that, my memories switch from ones of loving and laughing to ones of incrimination and bitterness.

I take a moment to be selfish and consider if doing this would be what is best for me.

Can I even face the living embodiment of my greatest regret?

❦

The table vibrates under my tapping fingers and the sound of a melody I'm working on fills my ears. With my headphones on and a cap pulled down low over my eyes, people are paying me no attention.

I'm confident my presence in New York has gone unnoticed so far. I've learned that is one of the perks of doing things on the spur of the moment. No one knows your plans, so there's no one to spill the beans. However, the reality is, I have no idea how many camera lenses might be waiting for me out there, hidden away. But from my booth in the back corner of this cozy diner I have a clear view of the entrance, while remaining obscured from the large front window. Concealed from public consumption.

Picking up my pen, I scrawl a couple of lines of lyrics, frustrated that this song doesn't seem to be coming together. The melody woke me up a few nights ago and I had to quickly grab my guitar and record it with my phone to make sure I didn't lose it. I've spent the last two days traveling and trying to work on the lyrics, but the words aren't coming.

Scribbling out the last line I wrote, I slam the pen back on the Formica surface and scrub my hands across my face. Removing my headphones, I gulp down the last of my coffee and check my watch.

Charlie refused to give me Wyatt's address or phone number, agreeing only to give me the name of this diner that she frequents, which turned out to be her aunt's. My ass has been planted in this booth all morning and I feel my frustration with Charlie rise, but before my temper has a chance to ignite, I remind myself that as far as this story goes, I'm the bad guy. I don't get to be pissed.

The door clatters open, bringing with it a gust of frigid air and a sound I never thought I would hear again.

My eyes are fixed on the laughing redhead and I shadow her movement with my eyes as she makes her way across the diner, falling into a booth with a chatty pink-haired girl who hasn't stopped talking since they entered.

I spend the next few minutes watching her without

one damn ounce of shame, reacquainting myself with all of her little quirks. The way she can't keep her hands still, constantly touching, gesturing, grasping. The shake of her head and roll of her eyes when she is amused. All of her little mannerisms that I never thought I'd get to see again. I watch it all, captivated, memorizing this new version of the girl I loved.

I wish I could say I waited. Or, that I tried to wait until she was alone. For a moment where my presence wouldn't throw her carefully constructed world into a tailspin. But it would be a lie. Because being in the same room as her, without being able to touch her was just too damn hard.

Pushing up from the table, I stride purposefully over to her table, trying to convey the confidence that seems to have deserted me, right when I need it the most.

A fraction of a second before her friend spots me, her eyes widening, I see Wyatt's back straighten as though a jolt of electricity has shocked her, and I see her wary eyes search the room.

I force my feet to stop at their table. The urge to run is sudden and all-consuming, but when she looks up and her gaze meets mine, a sense of home fills me.

We stare at each other wordlessly. The air is thick with tension and I try to read her reaction, but it's a shock to realize that I am no longer fluent in Wyatt Monroe.

"Hey, guitar-boy." A wry voice has my head spinning toward the friend, who apparently is a feisty one. "Can we help you?"

I slide my gaze back toward Wyatt, waiting for her to say something. When she doesn't, simply continuing to look at me with an expression that screams confusion, I step up.

"Just wondered if I could have a word with Wyatt."

Pink's eyes jump between the two of us, trying to read the situation, and I get a few more seconds to admire Wyatt before I'm shut down, ruthlessly.

"You know what?" She taps a finger to her mouth as though deep in thought. "Usually I'd say that sounds like a grand idea, but it doesn't look like she wants to talk to some random stranger who approaches us creepily in a diner. Mmm 'kay? Run along now." Her lips form a hard line and I get the sense she's going to be tough to win over, which causes me to shake my head and give her my trademark smirk.

"I promise you, I'm not a random, creepy stranger. I'm—"

"I know," she cuts me off. "You're Flynn Maguire, and you probably don't hear this a lot, but I couldn't give two flying fucks. Buh bye." She waves me off like I'm an inconsequential bug, and my smirk grows to a full-blown grin.

I think I like this one.

"Not what I was going to say, Pink." I bathe my tone in sarcasm, a language I'm sure she understands. "I was going to say I'm her—"

"Flynn, don't." Wyatt's anxious voice interrupts, but it's too late.

"—husband."

CHAPTER THREE

WYATT

"*H*oly fudging croc sucker."

You can say that again.

"Come again?"

"Come again," Cassidy mimics Flynn's question with a savage smirk before her expression morphs into one of indignation. "Don't judge me, I have kids, I can't swear anymore, donkey dick."

I watch their exchange through wide eyes, but I hear nothing over the sound of blood rushing to my brain. The thrum of my heartbeat.

Shit. Shit. Shit.

My eyes find Flynn's and I see the exact moment he realizes his mistake and all I can feel is shame. Because it never would have occurred to him that he was my dirty little secret.

But that is only because he was too busy making sure I was his.

"You're married?" Cassidy aims this directly at me.

"To Flynn Maguire?" My stomach drops a little farther with every accusatory word.

"Look, if you don't mind, Wyatt and I have some shit we need to talk abo—"

"Uh uh, pipe down, Romeo, this doesn't concern you. Wyatt?" She does that thing where she quirks a single eyebrow. It's always fascinated me how she does that. I've spent an embarrassing number of hours in front of the mirror trying to replicate that withering look.

I was not successful.

"It was a long time ago." The hesitance in my voice is embarrassing and I can see the confusion all over Cassidy's face. This is not the Wyatt she knows. The person she has laughed and cried with for eight years. This is the version of me I swore would never see the light of day again.

And she won't, I quickly decide. Straightening my back and ignoring Cassidy's curious stare, I lift my eyes to meet Flynn's, prepared to blow him off and send him on his way. But when my gaze clashes with his, my breath catches in my throat as a tsunami of relief washes over me.

He's here.

He's here and I have missed him so damn much.

Tears prickle behind my eyes and I swallow hard, resisting the almost overpowering instinct to leap up and wrap myself around him. To touch him and make sure he's real. But clarity prevails, and I take note of his hunched shoulders and guarded expression. I remember the pain on his face the last time I saw him, and I realize that I don't deserve the luxury of his reassurance. The bad guy never does.

Instead I give him a tense smile.

"This isn't a very good time." I incline my head slightly toward Cass. "Maybe we could get together tonight?" The words come out in a rush and even though I know I should send him on his way, the need to talk to him is suffocating.

A whoosh of air escapes him and his face smooths as though he's relieved at my suggestion.

"Yeah, that sounds great. Just tell me where, and I'll be there." The lilting sound of his Irish accent fills me with such familiarity and I allow myself a moment to remember how I used to love closing my eyes at night, falling asleep to the sound of his voice. His accent isn't as pronounced as it once was, and I feel the regret of the years I've lost with it, with him, intensely.

I notice a table to our right, full of teenage girls, watching us curiously. Their brows furrowed as though trying to figure out where they know Flynn from. God, he must hate that.

"How about my place? I think privacy would be a good idea."

A smirk flits across his mouth. "You always did like keeping me to yourself."

My eyes narrow, but a quiet laugh from across the table reminds me that we are not alone.

"Not the way I remember it but play it that way if you have to. Give me your phone." I hold my hand out in anticipation. Flynn slides his cell out of his back pocket without hesitation, placing it in my hand. His fingertips gently nudge me, and I can feel the pink blush bloom across my face.

Lighting up his screen, I look at him expectantly. Exasperation courses through me when he just stares back, wordlessly.

"I need your passcode."

"You know my passcode, Wyatt." His voice is quiet, but firm and my heart picks up speed when I realize what he's saying. He still uses my birthday.

Heat floods through my body and the vinyl of the seat sticks to my skin uncomfortably as I wiggle around, trying to get comfortable under his intense gaze. Giving my head a quick shake to clear it, I enter my phone number and send myself a text so I have his.

"I'll message you my address later, and you can come around seven."

"Okay." He opens his mouth and I think he's going to say something else, but instead, he simply closes it and stares at me for a beat before turning around and walking out without another word.

I watch him leave, a million thoughts and questions suddenly racing through my mind and I kick myself for not asking them. Tonight, I promise myself.

"You." Cassidy's voice gains my attention and I turn to face her, finding an accusing finger pointed my way. "Have a lot of explaining to do."

"I am going to kill you," Charlie's answering sigh rings through my phone. I have been trying to get a hold of her all afternoon, as soon as I raced out of the diner with promises to Cassidy that I would explain everything trailing behind me. Five hours later she has finally taken my call. No doubt hoping my temper would have had time to cool down.

Unfortunately for her, she's all out of luck.

"I'm not arguing with you about this, Reeses." I ignore her use of my childhood nickname. "I did what I thought needed to be done and I'm not going to apologize for it." Charlie's voice is resigned.

"What did you tell him?" I'm recalling every confession I made to her earlier in the week, and I'm mortified at the idea of her giving up my secrets to Flynn. Shamed that after everything I did to him, he should be expected to feel sorry for me.

"Nothing. Christ, what kind of friend do you think I am?"

I pace around my tiny apartment, bumping into furniture, my hand tensing around the phone.

"Well, you told him something. How else did he end up ambushing me at Monroe's?"

"I only told him—" She cuts off and I hear someone in the background calling her name.

"Where are you?"

"At work." Her voice lowered to a whisper.

"It's Saturday, why are you working?"

"We're preparing for depositions on Monday. Look, I need you to listen to me." I hear the sound of air rushing by and I imagine Charlie striding purposefully down a hallway, probably toward some bland conference room, ready to conquer. "You need to talk to him.

You both need this. It's been almost ten fucking years and you're both still so wrapped up in your own pain. You need to apologize to each other and forgive." She pauses, and I hear the hush of murmured voices in the background. "You need to forgive each other and your-selves. Then, maybe, you can both finally move forward. I have to go, I'll call you tomorrow. I love you."

Just like that, she's gone. I groan loudly into the empty space of my apartment, allowing my frustration and, if I'm completely honest, my fear to have a voice.

I go back to pacing around the room, bumping into furniture occasionally, cursing and considering for the millionth time that it's time to find somewhere bigger to live. The second hand on the gaudy pink clock, that hangs above my bed, ticks over loudly. A constant reminder that time is always moving forward, whether we want it to or not.

Needing something to soothe my mind and heart for the next couple of hours, I drag my comfortable armchair over in front of the picture window and settle myself in, sketchbook on my legging-clad lap and char-coal pencil in hand.

As always, my mind empties as soon as the pencil begins scratching over my notepad and I allow the feel of the paper and pencil to calm me.

My career illustrating children's books has picked up over the last few years and that, combined with the occasional artwork I commission, keeps me busy. If I'm honest, more busy than I would like at times.

It has been a few weeks since I dedicated any time

to my art, the work I create for myself, not a paycheck, and my hand races over the page, images coming to life faster than I can even form them in my mind.

My hands become increasingly black as I use them to smudge and shade and when I finally start to see the piece come together, I pull back, startled.

A loud knock on the door shocks me further and I jump up, body tense, and slam my sketchpad closed. On my way to answer the door, I stuff it under a pile of junk mail on the kitchen counter.

The door rattles again just as I reach it, but I take a moment before opening it. I have no idea how to prepare myself for this conversation, this meeting. No idea, really, how to be around Flynn anymore. There are days I don't even recognize myself anymore, I hate to imagine how disappointed he is going to be when he discovers the person I have become.

Shaking my head, I take a final deep breath and pull the door open.

He's there, leaning against the doorframe, his thick arms crossed over his chest. A blue cap is pulled down low over his dark brown hair, dark stubble covering his strong jaw and dark brown eyes lazily caress every inch of me. He is the epitome of tall, dark, and dangerous and when my pulse immediately starts racing, it hits me how much trouble I might be in.

"Took your time." A belligerent smirk lifts his lip. "You considered leaving me out here, didn't you?"

I take a minute, allowing my gaze to wander over his form, admiring the way his worn, faded jeans hug his long legs and the simple black tee he's wearing stretches over his broad chest, before I shrug my shoulders in what I pray is an indifferent manner. "It occurred to me, not gonna lie. You should probably come in before I change my mind."

His eyes meet mine and I can feel the challenge in them. The familiar war of wills that had always been our normal. Before I realize what I'm doing, I begin to close the door in his face, enjoying the look of surprise for a brief moment before the door blocks him from sight.

Just as it's about to shut, a hand reaches in and a loud curse sounds when the door clamps his hand against the doorframe. He pushes in, squeezing his large frame through the tiny space, glaring at me.

"Smartass."

I turn and follow him, watching while he takes in the small apartment. I refuse to let my eyes wander to his perfect ass, but just the thought of it reminds me of long, slow thrusts, my hands desperately clawing, trying to bring him deeper.

Giving myself a mental bitch slap, I take a step forward and point toward the small loveseat. "Sit. Do you want anything? I don't have any beer, but I think I have some vodka left."

He stops in front of the sofa and looks back at me. His face contorts into an expression of humor laced with pain, and my chest seizes with an unexplained pain.

"We gonna need alcohol for this?"

My hand that had been reaching for the refrigerator door, stops mid-air.

"I guess I just kind of assumed." Again, memories slap me up the side of my head. "Seems to me, most of our conversations after—" My throat closes, and I struggle to continue, tugging on the hem of my oversized sweatshirt nervously. "I just remember needing a lot of alcohol."

Flynn scrubs his hands across his face and flops down on the seat.

"I remember." His voice is sadder than I remember. "Coffee would be good. I haven't been sleeping well."

Nodding, I set about making some. Strong, black coffee for him and something much more palatable for me, full of sugar and caramel creamer. I try to ignore the awkwardness that blankets the air between us, but it's really all I can think about. My movements are stilted, and I don't remember ever feeling so uncomfortable in my own skin. It doesn't help that his eyes have not left me the entire time. I feel them as surely as I would feel his touch and it's making me incredibly self-conscious.

"Here you go." After what feels like roughly seventy-three hours, but was more likely less than five minutes, our drinks are finally ready. I grab the two mugs and begin to move toward him, embarrassingly captivated by the small smile he gives me. Not watching where I am going, my elbow bumps the pile of junk mail from earlier and I watch in horror as it, along with my sketchpad, crashes to the floor.

I turn around and the coffee mugs make a loud bang as I dump them on the counter. Coffee sloshes over the sides and my hands sting from the burn, but I quickly try to get to the spilled puddle and snatch up my book.

My heart slams into my chest when I turn and see Flynn already kneeling down, gathering everything up.

It feels as though he's moving in slow motion and the needle of despair pricks harder when I see his eyes light up at the sight of my sketchbook. He never could stop himself from looking, no matter how many times I told him to fuck off.

I watch him stand and straighten, I want to scream at him to stop, but I'm paralyzed, completely unable to move or speak.

His large hand begins turning the pages. I notice how the charcoal smudges his fingers slightly as they trace lightly over the drawings. His jaw relaxed now and his expression curious.

I watch this all dispassionately, knowing what's to come. Dreading it.

I know it as soon as he reaches my sketch from earlier. I can see it in the way his body tenses, his hand stilling. I watch as his eyes widen briefly, before closing tight, shutting me out.

"I'm sor—"

"Don't. When did you draw this?" His voice is tight, harsh, and I know that any hope we had of sorting this shit out tonight has disappeared.

"Tonight." I slip my mask on, falling into old habits, removing any emotion from my voice and face.

Flynn is the complete opposite, his face a riot of conflicting emotions and I prepare for him to storm out. For this to be my last memory of him.

"Wyatt?" The sound of his broken voice draws my gaze back to him and I can't help but admire the rawness of him.

"Fuck!" he roars out and before I can make any sense of what is going on, he is bearing down on me, a look of exquisite torture painted on his face.

CHAPTER FOUR

FLYNN

It's us. Or at least it's the us we could have been.

Would have been, if it weren't for me.

My mind is racing, and I try to take in the image in front of me. It's this room, sketched in remarkable detail right down to the threadbare rug in front of the sofa. Wyatt is seated in front of an easel by the window, but instead of looking at the view in front of her, her eyes are turned to watch the people behind her, on the couch. I'm there. My old, much-loved guitar, the one I rarely play anymore, on my lap and my fingers strumming the strings. Her imagery is so vivid I can feel the peace that settles over me when I get lost in creating.

But it's the person drawn to my left that has me unable to breathe. A young girl, with long, dark hair that falls down her back. The same back that is leaning against me at an angle. She's the right age and I know without a shadow of a doubt who it is.

Carys.

"I'm sor—"

She's apologizing? She's fucking apologizing for being heartbroken. To the person that broke her?

"Don't." My voice is harsher than I intended, but goddammit. I wanted her to be okay. I needed her to be okay. "When did you draw this?"

She's not okay.

"Tonight."

I tear my eyes away from the sketch I wish was our reality and I glance at her. Her face is blank, the same expression I was faced with for days upon months, all of which seemed indeterminately endless.

I thought by leaving I would be helping her. If she didn't have to face the person responsible for our daughter's death, she could move on. She could stop worrying about trying to forgive me and just let herself grieve.

Because God knows, I don't deserve her forgiveness.

"Wyatt?" Her impassive eyes twist my gut painfully. "Fuck!"

I can't stop myself from striding toward her, desperate to get my hands on her. Grabbing her hand, I pull her into me and wrap my arms around her tightly.

"I'm sorry. I'm so fucking sorry."

I repeat the words over and over until I feel her relax into me. I keep saying them until I feel her arms lift and cling on to my back, clawing at me and pulling me even closer. I continue saying the words to her until I feel her body shaking with the sobs of a pain so intense that only the truly unlucky will ever experience.

Only then do I stop.

※

"I imagine her as a mini you. I think she would have been serious and snarky." Her voice is sad. "Sometimes, I dream about her and she has the same evil glint in her eye that you get when someone is being exceptionally stupid." Wyatt's face lights up. "And you would think that would get her into all sorts of trouble but, unlike you, she would have the charm to win people over."

"Hey, I'm charming." I lean forward, enjoying the familiar roll of her eyes, and carefully place my mug on the coffee table, before giving her a broad smile, enjoying the ease between us.

There was definite awkwardness after Wyatt's breakdown. I could see how vulnerable she felt, and I know her well enough to know how much she hates that. But I've witnessed her defenses drop over the last few hours, she has morphed into the girl I loved all of those years ago, so perhaps it was exactly what she needed. What we both needed.

Forced to face our mutual demons, we have been talking about things we should have discussed all those years ago. Confessions and shattered dreams that broke us, now feel like they could be our absolution.

"I think she would have looked like you." I reach over and tug a lock of her hair, wrapping it around my finger loosely. "Hair as beautiful as the most stunning sunset and eyes that glitter like emeralds."

"Ugh." She rolls her eyes. "That was corny as fuck. I swear you used to be better than that."

A loud laugh rolls through my body and it sounds so foreign to my own ears.

"I never talk about her." Wyatt's declaration sobers me. "I just don't know how, you know?" She glances up at me and my smile fades to a slight grimace.

"Yeah. I get it." I consider my words carefully. I'm so fucking desperate to reassure her, the need to fix her as fierce today as it was all those years ago. "I feel like actually saying the words is going to permanently wreck me. Like, if I admit how broken I am, there will be no hope of ever being okay."

She's nodding, a bright sheen to her eyes as she watches me intently.

"Yeah." The word is a gentle whisper and she closes her eyes and roughly rubs them. "I felt that way for so long. If I could just pretend it didn't hurt, then it wouldn't." I hear her sigh and watch her chest rise and fall with the deep intake of breath. "I've always drawn her. Whatever age she would have been, that's how I would draw her, and it always brought me a certain amount of peace. But it's not enough anymore. Not talking about her is becoming more painful. Some-times I need to say her name, just to remind myself that she wasn't a dream."

She reaches over and places her hand on my knee, squeezing gently.

"Do you ever worry that she's watching us, and she

doesn't realize how much we love her? How sorry we are?"

My hand finds its way to hers. "No. Carys knows. She has to."

She huffs out a small laugh and leans back into the large, overly stuffed cushions.

"You're right." Her long legs slide up and under her ass before she turns to fully face me with an expression I can't quite place.

"I'm sorry for what I said to you. It was cruel, and I have spent every day since regretting it. I don't blame you for leaving." Her shoulders lift in a small shrug. "How could you stay after that? I was so wrapped up in my own pain that I didn't have room to care about yours as well. Oh God." She curls into herself slightly and covers her face with both hands. "I sound like such a bitch."

I reach across and gently pull her hands away.

"You sound like a mother who lost her child. Christ, we were so fucking young, we did what we had to do to survive it the best we could. I don't blame you for anything, Cherry."

Her eyes soften, and I remember when she looked at me like that on the regular.

"I miss that name. I feel like she's who I was before it all happened." Her teeth find her full lower lip and she bites down. "Sometimes I want to be her again so badly, it's a physical pain."

I want to drag her to me, feel her body against mine and convince her that she will always be that person to me. But we're not there yet.

Yet.

"There's not a damn thing wrong with who you are right now. Look at everything you've done over the last ten years." I gesture to the photo collage she has created along an entire wall of her apartment. "You've traveled, you've built friendships with people who would kick my ass if given half the chance." I grin as I remember my run-in with her friend at the diner. "And, from what I hear, you're killing it with the whole artist thing."

"From what you hear? How are you hearing things about me? Ahhh." She rolls her eyes. "Charlie."

"Don't get pissy with her, I never really gave her a choice. I hounded her until she would tell me what I wanted to hear, just to get rid of me."

She laughs, and I feel an answering smile spread across my face. Wyatt Monroe happy is a sight to behold.

"It's good to know you haven't changed at all." Her lips purse slightly and her eyes narrow as she holds my gaze. "Despite you being a super famous rock god and all."

"Fuck that." I groan. "You make me sound like some douchey cliché."

"Weeelll, I mean, not that I've followed you or anything."

Yeah, my ass she hasn't. I'd bet my last dollar she's followed me just as closely as I've followed her. She just had the luxury of being able to do it through the media and not having to resort to bribery and demands of old friends.

"But according to the tabloids you are kind of a douchey cliché."

"They're all a bunch of assholes. I keep my shit to myself and so they create stories that are ten times worse than the worst fucking thing you or I could ever imagine, just because they're pissed you're not giving them anything." Tension is pulsing through me at the thought of her believing all the fucking ridiculous things written about me over the years.

"Whoa, whoa, whoa." Her hands are thrown up. "I was just messing with you, I know that stuff is bullshit."

"Yeah?" My shoulders relax slightly.

"Yeah. I mean you used to go out of your mind if another guy even flirted with me, there's no way you're sharing your girl in a threesome. Even if that guy did win an Oscar."

She winks at me. Fucking smartass.

"I mean, okay, maybe they weren't all lies." I do my best to sound self-conscious, but it takes all my restraint not to lose it at the small pout playing on her lips.

"I don't need to hear about all the women you've fucked, 'kay, Irish?"

"Jealous?" I challenge.

"Pfft, please. I'm hardly going to be jealous of all the plastic Barbie dolls you've been attached too. Besides." Her eyes narrow evilly. "I get laid plenty, I don't need to concern myself with your sex life."

Okay, and the tension is back.

"Maybe we don't talk about this." My hand reaches up and I try to knead the stress from my neck.

"Good call." She grins at me. "I have to admit, I'm surprised you just showed up here. I would have thought you didn't go anywhere without an entourage, these days."

"Really? We both know I don't like people enough to deal with that shit." I shift in my seat, moving closer to her, just enough so she doesn't notice.

"Yeah, that's true." She snort-laughs and it captivates me in a way that a snort really shouldn't. "I guess I just didn't think you would be able to walk around the streets unnoticed, that's all."

"You'd be surprised what I can get away with." I wink at her which causes her to roll her eyes. "No, seriously though. People are in their own world, living their own lives. They don't expect to see the person whose music they sing along to, in Target, you know? If they do recognize me, more often than not they convince themselves they're mistaken. I'm not gonna lie though, I don't test the theory out too often, these days."

"Yeah, I can see that. So..." She leans slightly forward, her brow raised. "Target, huh?"

"Fuck, yeah. Never trust anyone who doesn't love Target, Cherry. Words to live by, swear to God."

Her laugh rings through the air, lightening the mood and we launch into conversation, sharing our lives and our secrets. Everything we've missed over the years. I'm hurting for every drop of information she's giving me like a junkie craving his next fix.

My eyes are fixed on her mouth as she tells me how she got started illustrating children's books and it takes me a minute to realize she asked me a question.

"What?" I can't even try to hide my distraction. All I can think about is how soft her lips look and how much I want to taste her.

"Are you even listening to me?"

Shit, she sounds pissed. Tearing myself away from that mouth, I do my best to focus on what she's saying.

"Are you shitting me? Of course I am, Christ, when did you get so needy?"

"Fuck you, Irish. You were so not listening to me." She giggles.

That giggle. Fuck. Me.

"You helped out a friend on a college assignment, illustrating a children's book she wrote. Her professor passed it along to a friend of hers who is a children's author and she contacted you. Then you got contacted by a bunch of her author friends and so it began." I intone in a bored voice. "Did I miss anything?" Jesus, I hope I didn't miss anything.

"Ugh, fine. Maybe you were listening." She shrugs. "But I coulda sworn you were too busy thinking about kissing me."

My heart thunders in response to her words and a sharp pain cuts through my shoulder. Am I having a fucking heart attack?

"You would let me?" The old Flynn, who was one half of Wyatt and Flynn, would never have needed to ask. This Flynn, with his ass seated on this sofa across from Wyatt, he doesn't entirely know anymore, needs to ask.

"Probably. But it doesn't matter, I guess. Turns out you were listening, so I guess I was imagining things." She stifles a fake yawn. "I didn't realize it had gotten so late, we should probably call it a night."

I glance up at her ugly-ass clock—pink, Christ, this woman—and I'm surprised to see it's after two in the morning. But, if she thinks she's getting rid of me after that little comment, she's got another thing coming.

"Yeah, maybe we should."

The hint of disappointment that flashes over her face is the only encouragement I need.

Leaning forward, I grasp her neck and pull her toward me, my mouth finds hers and my tongue traces along her bottom lip, savoring the taste, still so familiar, even all these years later.

She groans, and I use the opportunity to slip my tongue in her mouth, the feel of hers sliding against my own has my cock hardening painfully.

I imagined tonight going a lot of ways. Her standing me up. Her telling me in no uncertain terms how she felt about me tracking her down. Her hand finding its way across my cheek.

I can honestly say I never considered this.

She moves against me, pushing me back against the couch and her mouth starts trailing soft licks along my jaw. When she slides her leg over my lap to straddle me, her pussy grinds along my cock causing my head to fall back, a loud groan rolling through me from deep within my chest.

My hands grip the cushion beneath me. I want to touch her so fucking bad, to slide into her pussy and thrust slowly, deeply. The way she always liked it. Instead, I'm imagining the look on her face tomorrow when this becomes just one more regret in our story.

She pulls away from me, eyes glazed over, her hips still rolling over my dick in the most perfect way. Her hands find their way into my hair and she pulls my face toward her until we are only inches away.

"Stop overthinking this." Kiss, hip roll, moan. "I want this. Now, let's see what you've got, Irish."

CHAPTER FIVE

WYATT

My words are like a red rag to a bull. Any trace of self-control evaporates and all I can say is thank-fucking-god. This is probably the worst idea I've ever had, but I want this. Him. I may even need it.

He surges forward with a ferocity that should frighten me. Instead I feel safe and wanted. Like this man would kill for me if he had to. Once upon a time that would have been true, but right now I'll settle for this moment of false refuge.

His hands thread through my hair, pulling me where he wants me. He never felt the need to be gentle with me and I love the desperation that is ingrained in his every touch. Love the heat that blazes along my skin after every contact.

Our mouths move against each other and ten long years of need is making it difficult to hold back. He's making these soft grunts, every time his tongue finds mine and I can't believe I'd forgotten how good this is.

How intensely I have always craved the sensory over-load that accompanies sex with Flynn Maguire.

How am I going to walk away from this?

"Baby." His hands move down my body, gripping my hips and grinding me against him. "You want to ride me so I can get my mouth on those tits or you want me to bend you over and fuck you from behind?" He leans down and kisses my neck before sucking hard, almost to the point of pain.

"Are you giving me a hickey?" I can't disguise the horror in my shriek as I push away from him and punch his shoulder as hard as I can. "You asshole!"

A quiet chuckle vibrates through his chest and he pulls me back in for a kiss, this time slow and delicious as though we have all the time in the world. Just when I think I'm about to come from the taste of him alone, he breaks away and lightly caresses my bottom lip with his thumb.

"Wyatt?" His voice is quiet and rough, as though he's about to reveal a dangerous secret and I automatically lean into him, needing to hear his confession.

"You about ready to sit on my dick, 'cause I need to be inside you like right fucking now."

"Ugh." A slap to his chest this time. "What happened to romance? You suck!"

"Not right now, but later, I promise."

His smirk is infuriating, and I would be more than happy to continue telling him off if the sight of his hands working his zipper open wasn't so distracting.

My hands fall to my side and I watch, captivated, as the zip slowly lowers, revealing a light trail of hair and nothing else. I keep watching as his large hand, God, I always loved his hands, lowers and I have to bite my lip to stifle a groan when he pulls his cock free, jerking himself roughly.

I should move. I should slide to my knees and take him in my mouth. He's the only guy whose dick I've actually enjoyed having in my mouth, so I have no explanation as to why I'm frozen to the spot. Other than the fact I'm enjoying the view too damn much.

"Baby?"

"Hmmm?"

"You good?"

"Mmmhmm."

A chuckle vibrates through him and I force my eyes to meet his.

"What?"

"Come here." His voice is demanding and snaps me out of my lusty haze.

"Wait." I hop up off his lap and make quick work of removing my leggings and panties. As I lift my sweat-shirt over my head, I see Flynn dragging his jeans off and the persistent throb in my clit intensifies.

Sliding back onto him, I press myself against him, desperate to get as close as possible. His arms immediately wrap around me, unclasping my bra and as soon as it drops to the floor, his mouth is on me, his tongue teasing my nipple and then he bites down deliciously hard, drawing a loud moan from me.

My hands tangle with his t-shirt, pulling it up and off. I flatten myself against him, my breasts cushioned against his chest and the contrast of our bodies intoxicates me. His hard to my soft. I know that regret will most likely find me tomorrow, but right now all I can do is surrender.

The feel of his mouth on the curve of my neck causes me to grind on him, and there is no finesse, no skill. My thighs instinctively tighten around him every time the head of his cock teases my clit and his hands are clutching my ass, dragging my wetness along his hard length over and over, torturing us both.

When his mouth finds mine, I lean forward and my ass lifts, giving him the room he needs to place his cock at my entrance. I feel him push the tip in, stretching me in the most perfect way. I thread my hands through his hair and with his tongue moving with my own, his hands pinching my nipples, I press down until he is fully seated inside me.

So. Fucking. Deep.

So. Fucking. Perfect.

He breaks our kiss, letting out a roar. "Jesus Christ." His accent is more pronounced, his voice ragged and strained. I roll my hips, the need to move faster, to pull him in deeper, urging me on. All I can hear is the sound of us. Flynn's harsh grunts as he pushes up forcefully, meeting me thrust for thrust. My low moans as his thick cock hits the perfect spot within me. The gentle sound of our bodies sliding against each other in an act that is far from gentle.

It's desperate, needy fucking. It's us taking everything from each other that we've missed these past years. Taking everything from each other that we're going to miss in the coming ones.

"So, so good," I hiss. "Don't stop, don't stop, don't stop."

He buries his head in my neck with a choked laugh. "Not gonna stop, baby. You gonna come for me?"

"Yes, yes, yes, yes." I whisper the words on repeat, completely unaware, and I feel myself tighten around him, coming so hard my vision blurs momentarily.

I feel my body go languid, and I lean against Flynn, allowing him to take control. His hands grip my hips painfully and he thrusts up vigorously. Sweat that is surprisingly cool on my skin, drips from his forehead onto my shoulder and there is something so incredibly raw and beautiful about this moment.

Flynn loses control, pushing himself deep within me and I feel him come at the same moment he releases a loud, animalistic groan.

Right there in the midst of the sounds and scents of what could only be described as dirty, crass sex, I feel like I've come home.

❦

The soft glow of the sunrise is starting to peek through the curtains. Flynn's talented fingers are playing with my hair and I can feel sleep starting to drag me under.

"I have to leave in a couple of hours, Cherry. I wish I didn't have to, but I need to be back in LA by midday."

"Mmmhmm." God, his voice is so soothing, how had I forgotten that?

"Wyatt?"

"Mmmm?"

"Promise me you're not going to regret this?"

"Okay." I fall asleep with his fingers tangled in my hair and his lips on my temple.

❧

"So, explain."

I stare at the two faces looking back at me. One glaring, one curious.

My mouth opens, but when words fail to come, I clamp it shut again. I'm still reeling from my encounter with Flynn last night and I feel unprepared for this interrogation. I almost refused Cassidy's demand to meet today, only relenting when I realized it would just make matters worse.

"Look, Red, I don't know about Skyeballs here, but I'm pissed." She pushes her giant caramel frappe away and crosses her arms over her chest with a haughty pout. "We're supposed to be your best friends, so explain to me how you think it's okay, in any universe, for us not to know that you're married to a fucking rock star? How?"

"What I think Cass means is," Skye, sweet, sweet Skye who hates confrontation, interrupts, throwing Cassidy a pointed look. "We were surprised to find out you were married. And, maybe a little hurt you didn't feel like you could confide in us."

"That is not what I meant at all, Balls. I am pissed." Her blue eyes continue to glare at me.

"Okay, okay." I hold my hands up in defeat. "I am

the worst friend in the world, is that what you want to hear?"

"No!"

"Yes."

Their answers are simultaneous and force an unexpected laugh from my lips.

"It didn't have anything to do with trust, it was never about you, I promise." I can't stop my fingers from playing anxiously with the sugar packets and I'm seconds away from tearing one open and scattering sugar all over the table, just to keep them occupied, when a gentle hand covers my own.

"You don't have to tell us anything, Wyatt." Skye's eyes are full of compassion. "We all have things that hurt so much it feels impossible to put them into words."

This right here, this is why I love Skye Mackinnon.

"Okay, well, maybe you don't need to give us all the gory details." Cassidy sounds slightly remorseful. "But you have to tell us something."

I lean back in my seat, the plush velvet chair soft against my skin, grateful we're having this conversation at the quiet coffee slash book shop that Skye manages.

"I met him when I was fifteen." Deep breath. Breathe in. Breathe out.

"He had just moved from Ireland with his mom after his parents divorced. He was—" I search for the words to adequately describe him. "Quiet. But he had this presence, even then. He was hot as fuck, the answer to every rebellious teenage dream with his broody, bad boy musician thing." I smile at the memory. "Then he would open his mouth and every word was snide, sarcastic perfection delivered in the most exquisite Irish accent. I was screwed from the start. Never even had a chance."

"You were childhood sweethearts? Oh my God, that's so beautiful!" Skye swoons while Cassidy rolls her eyes at her enthusiasm.

"Anyway," I continue, anxious to get this story over with. "We began dating. When we turned eighteen, we ran off to Las Vegas and eloped, much to the horror of our parents. God, I still remember the reaming my parents gave us when we got home. My father threatening to end Flynn if we didn't annul the marriage. But we stood firm." I pause to take a sip of my coffee, mostly to give my hands something to do, before pushing on. "Our town in Texas was tiny, there were no opportunities for a musician or an artist, so we moved a couple of towns over. We thought we were so grown." I shake my head sadly. "We had no fucking clue."

"What happened?" Skye's gentle voice probes.

"I started going to art school and waitressing at night. Flynn taught guitar lessons during the day and played gigs at night. We had this tiny little one-bedroom apartment." I smile at the memory. "We were eighteen and had no doubt that every one of our dreams would come true. That we would make them come true. Then I got pregnant."

"Holy ducking plot twist!" Cassidy exclaims.

"Cass!" Skye hits her on the leg, narrowing her eyes and looking remarkably formidable.

"What?" she asks innocently. "I did not see a baby coming!"

I snort out an ironic laugh. "Well, that makes three of us."

"If you tell me that douchenugget tried to make you get rid of it, I will hunt him down and slice his dick off with the bluntest knife I can find."

"No, no, no. It was nothing like that. There was an accident." I clutch my coffee mug to my chest, needing the feel of something tangible beneath my fingers as tears threaten to fall. "I experienced some abdominal trauma and it caused severe placental abruption. Carys was stillborn at twenty-three weeks." I attempt to give them a reassuring smile, to let them know I'm okay, but their concerned expressions tell me I'm not successful.

"We struggled to cope. I was… angry. Very angry. I blamed him, he tried to help me, but I just couldn't—" I choke on the words. "I pushed him until he had no choice but to leave. When he finally did, I just shut down. Eventually my parents encouraged me to come out here, stay with my aunt, and start fresh. It took some persuading, but it was the best thing I ever did." This time my smile comes slightly easier. "I could breathe again. I started over. Started dreaming again. I built a new life and, for the most part, I've been happy."

I reach over and place my mug on the small round table positioned between our chairs, and slump down in my seat.

"I'm so sorry, Wyatt. I can't even imagine how awful that must have been."

"My heart is fucking breaking for you right now," Cassidy consoles.

I can't believe the relief that is overwhelming me right now.

"And I have so many questions," Cass continues.

Okay, that relief was short lived.

"Ask away." I sigh.

Cassidy and Skye exchange a look before turning to me expectantly.

"You never saw him again?"

"How has the press not found out about you?"

"Why didn't you get divorced?"

"What did he want yesterday?"

"Do you think you'll get back together?"

"How big is his dick?"

Skye's mouth drops, and I laugh loudly, the tension between the three of us easing.

"Cassidy!"

"Oh, please, like you weren't thinking it." She turns to me. "We're waiting, Red."

"Ugh, okay, let me see." I start checking their questions off on my fingers. "No, I never saw him again. He moved to LA and I moved here. I actually have no idea. Like I said, we're from a small town and we protect our own. I don't see anyone from home spilling our secrets. Plus, I'm sure they all assumed we got divorced. We never got divorced because, well, I didn't file because I couldn't face him, or what had happened, I suppose. I have no idea why he never did it." A shrug of my shoulders. "He came to see me because he heard I wasn't doing well. A friend of ours suggested he come, and we talk things through, finally try and make peace with each other." My heart drops at the next question. "No, we won't be getting back together. He left early this morning to go back home." I do my best to ignore the sense of loss I felt when I woke to an empty bed this morning, instead plastering on a cheeky grin. "And, it's big. Like, big, big." I hold my hands apart to give them a visual.

Skye loses it, giggling in embarrassment while Cassidy's eyes widen.

"Well, damn."

"Can I ask you something?" Skye's soft voice asks when we have all recovered.

"Sure, ask away."

"You said you weren't doing well? Why didn't you come to us?" I don't miss the hurt in her voice and I consider how to answer her.

"When I first met you, it was all still too raw. Moving here, while allowing me a fresh start, it also gave me the perfect opportunity to pretend it had never happened. I was so broken, but it felt good to be around people who had no idea." I shrug, helplessly. "By the time I realized I was stuck with the two of you, it was too late. The more time that went by, the harder it seemed. It just seemed easier to leave it in the past."

"Okay, Red, you're forgiven."

I glance over at Cassidy in surprise, watching as she nonchalantly sips her ridiculously sweet drink.

"That's it?" I don't even bother trying to disguise the surprise in my voice.

"That's it," Skye confirms firmly. "It was your story to tell whenever you were ready." Her hand finds mine and squeezes comfortingly. "Thank you for trusting us." She leans back in her seat, pulling her legs up and crossing them. "I do wish you and Flynn had a different ending though. That would be an incredible story."

I ignore the shot of pain that tears through me at her words. Try to forget the sensation of coming home that overwhelmed me last night. He's gone and it's for the best.

"Well, I'm sorry to disappoint, but that story is well and truly finished. There's no happily ever after in my future, babes. You'll just have to settle for your own."

Skye opens her mouth to say something but is cut off when my phone lights up and starts jumping around on the table between us. The name Flynn and a picture of us lying in bed last night, lighting up the screen.

Cassidy raises an eyebrow.

"You were saying?"

CHAPTER SIX

FLYNN

"What?" Her voice hisses through the line causing a smirk to find its way to my lips.

"What's with the attitude, Cherry? I'm just calling to say hi." I can practically hear her eyes roll.

"I'm busy, and you totally just ruined a point I was — Stop it, Cassidy!" I can hear muffled voices in the background and a chuckle escapes as I imagine her getting torn a new one by her friends for keeping our history a secret.

"I have to go."

The line goes dead before I have a chance to say anything. So, I do what any man in my position would do. Call back.

"Oh my God, what do you want?"

"You should get your phone checked, babe, the call just dropped. That can't be good." I don't even bother trying to hide the sarcasm.

"The call didn't drop, I hung up on you." She speaks

slowly, enunciating each word.

"Well, that was fucking rude."

A loud sigh hits my ear. "Just wait a second, yeah?"

I hear her murmuring an apology and then there are the sounds of movement. My name is called, and I hold my hand up to Jett, my drummer, indicating I need a few more minutes. He nods, and I watch him saunter away, joining the rest of my band in preparation for our soundcheck.

"Right." Her voice draws my attention. "I'm here, what's up?"

"Did you get my note?"

"I did, yes. Thanks for not waking me up. I would have had to kick your ass and I feel like that would have been a shitty way for the visit to end."

I laugh, grateful that she isn't making this as hard as she could.

"So, did you have an actual reason for calling or did your spidey senses tell you calling me right now would be just perfect?"

I ignore her sarcasm, everyone around me is starting to get antsy so I know I need to wrap this up quickly.

"Look, I'm going to be back in New York in a couple of weeks, so we're going out to dinner. I get in on the morning of the seventh, so keep that night free."

"Flynn, we need you, man." I glance back at Jett, nodding.

"Right, I've gotta go, talk soon."

"Wait, wait, wait!"

I catch her startled response right before I disconnect the call and a twinge of doubt settles deep in my stomach.

"What's wrong?"

"I don't think that's a good idea."

Shit.

"I think it's an excellent fucking idea, so how about you just take my word for it."

"Flynn," she says with a sigh, her voice all soft and troubled.

Turning my back on the hundred or so people all waiting for me, I duck into an empty corridor and lean against the brick wall, the cold seeping through to my skin.

"Wyatt."

Silence greets me.

"Talk to me, Wyatt. I'm not putting up with the no-talking bullshit."

"I'm glad you came to find me. Shit!" She groans. "That doesn't do it justice. I was in a horrible place and I will always be grateful to you for that visit. Just getting to talk about her—"

I hear her sniff on the other end of the line and my free hand subconsciously scrubs itself across my eyes.

"It felt good talking about her with you, I feel like we never did that, and I wish we had." Her voice lowers to just above a whisper and I have to strain to hear her. "I wish we had done a lot of things differently, maybe we could have survived."

"But we didn't." My voice is harsh, but for once I don't have to worry about how the other person will perceive me. Wyatt never shied away from my hard edges, never expected me to be anyone other than myself.

"No, we didn't."

I can hear the noise on the other side of the door, people racing around, excuses being made, and the voices are growing more agitated by the second.

"I fucked up back then. I made a shitload of mistakes, Wyatt, and I regret every single one of them. I let guilt take—"

"You have nothing to feel guilty for, Flynn."

"What I'm saying is"—I brush her comment off, we both know it's a giant pile of horsecrap—"that we need to leave the past where it belongs and focus on our future."

The line remains silent.

"You know, I remember you being chattier than this, Cherry."

"We don't have a future." Her voice is firm. It's her don't-mess-with-me voice. I remember it well. It usually preceded a three-hour-long fight that would end with us fucking each other senseless.

"Last night was amazing and I feel like we set things right. What we had never should have ended the way it did, and I feel like last night we gave ourselves the ending we deserved. But that's what it was, an ending."

"That's what you think, huh?"

A loud bang on the door scares the shit out of me and I slam on it yelling, "Just a fucking minute."

"I better go, Cassidy and Skye are waiting on me. Take care, okay?"

"Right," I rasp. "Wyatt?"

"Yeah?"

"You're wrong." Then I disconnect the call.

§.

"You coming to the party at Tucker Royal's tonight? I heard Raina's gonna be there."

Tucker Royal is one of the biggest assholes I have ever met, I don't care how many fucking awards he's won or how many millions of dollars his movies make. He will always just be a grade-A dickhead to me. As for Raina, the woman can suck a dick better than most, but she's also bat-shit crazy. You ever see that episode of *How I Met Your Mother* where they talk about the hot-to-crazy scale? It could have been written about Raina.

"Nah, I don't think so."

"Aw, c'mon, man!" Wes, who after joining my band a year ago, still holds the title of *new guy*, tries to convince me. He's laughably green and impressed by all the perks this lifestyle affords us.

"I told Brax I would stop by tonight, see the monster." The mention of Brax, my best friend and old bass guitarist, the guy he replaced but can never truly replace, shuts him right up.

"You've got interviews tomorrow, starting at eight, so be ready." My manager, Campbell, joins us, shoving a list of entertainment outlets at my chest. His usual frenzied energy is slightly subdued and when I look at him closer, I realize how tired he looks.

"I'll be ready. You good, man? You look like you could sleep for a fucking month."

He loosens his tie before scrubbing a hand over his face. "Yeah, just a situation turning out to be more difficult than I first thought."

"Should I be worried?" To be honest, I've never really paid much attention to what Campbell does. We have the perfect working relationship. My strength is writing and playing music. His strength is everything else.

"Have you ever needed to worry?" he questions sharply.

I hold my arms up with a low chuckle. "Point taken. You should take the night off though, go get some sleep."

"Yeah, I will after I'm finished here." He motions to the chaos behind him where an army of roadies are dismantling the set in record time. "Say hi to Brax and Mel for me."

"Will do." With that, I turn and make my way through the winding corridors of the auditorium, meeting two of my bodyguards at the exit door.

"What's it like out there?"

"Not too bad." Zane, the larger of the two and the head of my security, reassures me. "Maybe a hundred, but they're a pretty easygoing bunch. At least they were before they see you." He smirks.

"Giselle's out there though," Connor warns.

"Shit." Giselle Cross, owner of the blog *Giselle's Inside Scoop*. She knows everything from the last person you fucked to the type of laundry detergent you use, she has a fucking vicious mouth and the female equivalent of a hard-on for me.

I have no idea how she hasn't dug up the fact that I'm still married, but I sure as fuck am happy that she hasn't.

"Alright, let's get this shit show over with and get me to Brax's place."

I take my position behind Zane and Connor, slide my sunglasses down to block the glare from the flashing cameras and take a deep breath.

This is the part of my job I hate the most. I have no desire to have my picture splashed on the covers of magazines or to be on television. I just want to be a musician. Unfortunately, this is the shitty price I have to pay for people to hear what I create.

"Okay, ready." On my word, Zane pushes the door open and the crowd, who had seconds before been a quiet mass, turns into a hysterical mob.

The flashes from the cameras blind me despite my sunglasses. The crowd, mostly young girls, pushing to get past the barricades, scream shrilly until I feel like my eardrums are going to burst. It's an overwhelming barrage of sensations that prickle along my skin like a fucking nightmare. But, I suck it up and get to work. I sign autographs, pose for selfies, answer the most ridiculous fucking questions you can imagine, and I do it all with a grin on my face that hides the fact that I would literally rather be anywhere but here.

When I'm finally nearing the car and I can practically taste my freedom, I'm pulled up short by a quiet but commanding voice.

"I heard you were in New York for a few days, Flynn. Was it business or pleasure?"

I look up into Giselle's icy blue eyes and I swear to God I have never wanted to harm a woman before today, but the antagonistic expression she's wearing sets off all of my protective instincts. Make no mistake, my need to protect Wyatt is powerful.

"Just checking out some possible venues for some smaller gigs. Have a great night." I get a glimpse of her narrowing eyes at my brush-off before I'm ushered away to the waiting SUV.

I spend the twenty-five-minute drive to Brax's Pacific Palisades home going over everything I did in New York and kicking myself for being so careless. After my talk with Charlie, I just booked the first flight I could get and took minimal precautions to prevent getting recognized.

Getting to Wyatt had really been the only thing on my mind.

The large gates in front of Brax's impressive home open wide allowing us to enter and I spot Mel by the front door straight away.

Tiny, with a messy blonde bob blowing in the light breeze, she waits with a smile on her face and a wriggling toddler in her arms. As I step out of the car, Brax walks up behind them and whispers something in Mel's ear. The monster takes full advantage of her distraction and works his way free, racing to me faster than any two-year-old should be able to move.

"Billy! How's it going, little dude?"

He throws himself at my legs, clinging on, mumbling into my jeans.

"Hurry up and get your ass in here, it's two hours

past his bedtime and he point blank refused to go until he'd seen your ugly mug."

I laugh and throw Billy up into my arms, making my way inside. Mel wraps her arms around me, squeezing tight. This woman gives massive hugs for someone so little.

"It's so good to see you." She reaches across to take her son. "Okay, Billy Bug, it's time for bed."

Saying goodnight to the indignant toddler takes longer than you'd think but as soon as we're settled in the huge living room, bourbon in hand, I let out a sigh of relief. My eyes wander around the room taking in the comfortable furniture, an eclectic mix of Mel and Brax's different styles which somehow work together to turn this monstrosity of a house into a home.

"You ready to come back yet?" It's the same question I've asked every time I have seen him since he left the band last year, to work as a session musician.

His answer is the same as always. He laughs in my face.

"Not a hope in hell, asshole."

"C'mon, I pay so much better." He levels me with a look of pity. Yeah, money isn't a problem for Braxton Havenworth.

"Don't you miss seeing my face every day?" I lift my hand, glass in hand, and gesture toward myself.

"I get to see Mel's pussy every day, which is much higher on my list of priorities." He downs the rest of his drink in a single gulp. "You gonna tell me how it went, or are we going to play twenty questions?"

I watch him get up and pour himself another drink from the full bar in the corner of the room.

"It went well." I rest my head on the back of the sofa, letting my eyes close.

"Did you fuck her?"

I open one eye and squint at him. "What part of what I told you would make you think we would fuck?"

"The part where you've been stupid in love with her for as long as I've known you."

My head falls back on the couch, my eyes close once again and I ignore his question.

Brax is the only person I have ever confided in about my past. I met him in a tiny dump of a club. It was my tenth day in LA and I was trawling the bars and clubs, looking for any that would let me play. He was a rich, obnoxious asshole who was slumming it and I was a poor-as-piss, broken asshole looking for a break. We met, we drank, and we drunkenly confessed our greatest sins to each other never thinking we would see the other again.

At least that's what I had thought. Two days later he had tracked me down and offered me a regular gig at a club owned by one of his cousins.

"She thinks it was us saying goodbye," I snort out.

"Has she met you?" he asks incredulously, now settled back comfortably in the armchair across from me. "What are you going to do? Because I know there's no way your stubborn ass is giving up that easily."

I give him a sly grin. "Of course not. I have a plan, but I'm going to need your help."

WYATT

"How did you get this pass again?"

Cassidy, Skye, and I are standing in front of one of the fanciest day spas I have ever seen. Like, it-probably-costs-more-than-my-annual-salary-for-a-manicure type of fancy.

I turn to the girls, taking in their skeptical faces still staring at the beautiful handcrafted sign, *Serenity by Havenworth*. The understated elegance reeks of money and I am suddenly very nervous.

"I got an email saying I won it."

"Won it, how?" Even Skye isn't convinced.

"I don't know," I reply slowly. "It said I was the lucky winner of the contest from their grand opening celebrations or something."

"Did you enter a contest?" Cassidy sounds even more unconvinced than Skye. "I mean this doesn't seem like the kind of place that gives away prizes, you know?"

"I-I. Maybe? Look." My voice turns defensive. "I

rang them to confirm it and they had all of my details, so I must have."

People are rushing around us, jostling and bumping, as we stand like idiots in the middle of the sidewalk, all of us hesitant to take the first step inside.

"Okay, this is ridiculous. We're booked in for their Pamper Day package so let's get in there and get ourselves pampered." I take each of them by the hand, ignoring the dubious look they're exchanging and pull them inside.

Walking through the dark-tinted glass door is like entering another world. Sedate, instrumental music is playing quietly in the background, immediately giving you a sense of calm. The color palette is all warm and muted colors with greenery everywhere. It might actually be physically impossible to feel stressed out within these walls.

We approach the front desk in the cavernous foyer, where a petite raven-haired girl with huge blue eyes greets us warmly.

After taking my name, we all breathe a sigh of relief when she confirms the contest win.

"We have you booked in for a deluxe manicure, pedicure, and facial, followed by a full-body sea-salt scrub and massage. I hope you ladies have cleared your entire day," she coos. "You'll barely be able to walk by the time we are done with you."

"Not how I usually like to achieve that particular feeling, but let's see how we do."

I fight back a laugh at Cassidy's comment, instead turning back to Zen-Barbie.

"That sounds amazing, we're definitely ready."

We are led to a giant, luxurious change room where we're instructed to change into the plushest robe I have ever laid eyes on and a pair of cute little slippers.

"You can put your personal belongings in the lockers around the corner to your right, and I will be back in a few minutes," Raven-haired girl tells us in her most soothing voice.

"This place is so beautiful. Wyatt, I don't care how you got these passes, I'm just glad you did." Skye sinks down onto a gorgeous emerald-colored armchair, eyes closed with a completely blissed-out look on her face.

"I second that. This place is probably too fancy for pussy, so underwear on, yeah?"

Skye's eyes pop open and meet mine across the room.

"Yes, please keep your panties on, Cass, I beg you." Skye laughs.

Ten minutes later we are settled in massage chairs, vibrating away, each of us with a girl by our feet, silently treating us to the most decadent foot massage and I am in heaven.

"Have you heard from Flynn?"

How quickly heaven can become hell. I look across to Skye for help, but she averts her eyes, suddenly fascinated with the floral prints on the wall opposite us.

"No, I haven't." My response is terse, and I cross my fingers that she takes the hint.

"Maybe you should call him." Well, look at that. They clearly weren't crossed hard enough.

"Why would I do that?"

Cassidy snorts out a laugh. "Because he has a ten-inch porn star dick that I'm pretty sure belongs in the cock hall of fame. Plus, you know." She shrugs. "You're still in love with him."

It's possible, I told them too much.

"Ugh, it's not ten inches. That would be way too much of a good thing." I cringe. "And painful."

Skye and Cassidy exchange a loaded look and I realize I have to put a stop to this real quick.

"No, uh-uh, there will be no looks. I am not still in love with him. That would be ridiculous and just asking for trouble."

"Then explain why you slept with him," Cassidy challenges.

"And why in the entire time we've known you, you've never gone out with a guy more than six times." Et tu, Skye?

"I slept with him because—" I pause, why exactly did I sleep with him? It's all a confusing blur of sensation and emotion.

"Yeeees?"

"Because who says no to sex? That's crazy talk! And"—I turn to Skye—"I have absolutely gone out with men more than six times."

"Nope. Jonathan Sterk, three years ago. You went out with him six times. You slept with him on date five and then said he was too clingy and broke it off."

"You counted?" I can feel my face contort in horror.

"Before him, it was Mark McLean. You dumped him after five dates." Skye is completely unapologetic.

I am acutely aware that we are not alone, that there are three people in the room with us who are most likely hanging on every word we're saying because, well, why wouldn't you? But when I glance at each of the women working on our feet, they appear completely uninterested.

"I—" I am not sure how to continue, that's what I am. "Okay, you want the truth?" The need to purge myself of one of my last remaining secrets is suddenly overwhelming. I may not be able to tell them the real reason Flynn and I will never happen, but I can give them this confession. And what better place to do it than in a luxury spa, half-naked under a robe, surrounded by three complete strangers, right?

Right.

"No, we want you to feed us a line of bullshit, so we can feel good about you feeling good," Cassidy snarks. "Get your head out of your ass, Red."

Skye fixes me with a look of disbelief and I take a moment to both appreciate and resent my friends' support.

The perky blonde seated at my feet, who I note, has a big smile and kind eyes, uses her knuckles to press deep into the arch of my foot, causing my head to fall back on the chair and my eyes to close in ecstasy.

"If you're finished orgasming over there, you were about to finally share a little truth with us."

I reluctantly open one eye and squint over at her. "You make it sound like I'm a habitual liar." I pout.

"No, just a habitual omitter of the truth." She sticks her tongue out at me.

"Ignore her, we completely understand why you didn't tell us." Skye reaches out and gives my arm a gentle squeeze. "But we want you to be honest with us. You can trust us."

My stomach churns with the knowledge that I still haven't been completely honest with them. That there is one secret that will always be only for me. So, I'll give them this admission, they deserve that at least.

"I love him." My words are confident, even when my heart is not.

"We know."

"Cassidy!"

My laughter flows easily and does wonders for loosening the lump that was forming in my throat.

"People thought we were crazy when we eloped. Our graduating class even had a pool going on how long we'd last." I have to bite my lip when I remember how pissed Flynn was when he found out. Right before he placed a bet on us lasting eighty years. I guess I showed him.

"But I knew I would never love anyone the way I love him, and I was right. We've been apart for ten years, but when I think about my heart, it's him I think of."

The room is silent but for the noise of water sloshing around our feet and gentle relaxation music playing in the background. I get the unmistakable feeling that the girls tending to us are now fully invested in this conversation, but I'm beyond caring.

"Despite that, we didn't make it. And I don't blame him for leaving." I inhale sharply, pushing away those unwelcome memories. "I treated him so badly, but my heart was shattered, and my soul barely survived it. Loving him almost broke me and I won't let that happen again."

The room is still, a shroud of unhappiness hanging over all of us and a pang of regret over that last little lie hits me deep in the gut. I would absolutely risk that heartbreak again, for him. If things were different, I would take that chance again in a heartbeat.

Anxious to ease the tension, I am about to make a joke when Skye beats me to the punch.

"I call bullshit." She shakes her head emphatically. "You were basically a child. Everyone was totally right; you guys were too young to get married. Sure, if you hadn't lost Carys you might still be together, and you might be rock solid and could survive anything. But back then? Neither of you had the emotional maturity to deal with your loss, let alone keep a marriage together through it."

"Thanks for that, Dr. Phil." Cassidy turns to me. "She's totally right though."

"No," I press on confidently, the need to perpetuate the lie now obvious. "If I couldn't make it work with him, I can't make it work with anyone. As for him, what's that saying about madness and doing the same thing over and over? We tried, and we failed. Trying again would be insanity."

"You're an idiot. I love you, but you're being an idiot."

"Cass, that's not helpful," Skye chastises before turning her attention to me. "She's right though."

I groan. Loudly. "You both suck."

"Of course we do, that's what our men love most about us." Cassidy smirks. "But that's beside the point. I don't agree with you, like at all, but I do get where you're coming from. I think you owe it to yourself to try to salvage something though, even if it's just a friendship." Her blue eyes narrow thoughtfully. "Nobody else will ever be able to understand what you went through, do you really want to give that up?"

I consider what she's saying, only slightly distracted by the sensation of my heel being scrubbed to slough away the dry skin (seriously, why does that feel so good?).

"I think," I start slowly. "That friends would be too hard to manage." And for a moment I'm lost, remembering the days after we split in vivid detail. How I had to box away every single thing that reminded me of him, block him on social media. Even warn people not to mention him, because the tiniest reminder intensified the pain that was already too intense for me to cope with. I couldn't believe that in less than a year my life had completely disintegrated, and the responsibility fell solely on my shoulders.

"It would just hurt too much."

"That was fluffing amazing." Cassidy slips back into mom-mode as we make our way to the exit.

"Soooo good. I've already decided that Ben can get dinner tonight and deal with the kids." Skye sighs. "I am going to go soak in a bubble bath with a glass of wine and my Kindle."

"That sounds perfect," I practically moan.

"You two are boring as fudge. I've already made arrangements for my mom to take the kids and Mason is going to fuck me senseless. Now that is the perfect end to the perfect day."

I roll my eyes and glance at Skye, only to stifle a laugh when I see her considering Cassidy's suggestion.

"Miss Monroe, do you have a minute?"

I look over my shoulder to the reception desk where a different woman, who exudes the same serene air, is now working.

"We'll wait," Skye assures me.

"No, it's fine, you go. I'm in the opposite direction anyway. I'll get an Uber as soon as I'm done."

"If you're sure?"

"Absolutely, you go." We indulge in a round of goodbye hugs and I accept their thank-yous for today, but they have no idea how good it was for my soul. Sometimes only your girls will do and today was most definitely one of those times.

I approach the reception desk cautiously, suddenly worried and mentally calculating my bank balance in case we incurred some charges today that weren't covered by my prize.

"Today was incredible, I will absolutely be recommending you to everyone I can." I infuse my voice with enthusiasm, hopeful the day isn't about to go completely south.

"I'm so pleased to hear that." She smiles. "As part of

your prize you also won a bottle of wine, so if you wouldn't mind accompanying me to the restaurant?"

"Oh, of course, thank you so much."

I follow her through a wide hallway, her heels echoing on the marble floors as I take in the beautifully textured artwork lining the walls. The technique demonstrated is stunning and I am so distracted I almost run into the woman's back when she stops suddenly in front of the closed restaurant doors.

"Right through here, Miss Monroe, they'll take care of you inside." With that, she turns on her heel and makes her way back the way we just came.

A little off-balance from her abrupt departure, I push through the doors eager to collect my wine and get home, only to pull up short when the last person I expected to see is standing by the bar, an impatient look on his face.

"Jesus Christ, you took your sweet-ass time, Cherry."

CHAPTER EIGHT

Her eyes flare in surprise when she spots me and, for a second, I think she's going to turn and run. Instead, her face scrunches up, the way it does when she's pissed. So fucking cute.

"What are you doing here?" Her voice is demanding, immediately reminding me of other times she likes to demand things and just like that, I'm sporting a semi.

"I told you we were going to have dinner tonight." I shrug and push off from the bar. She stalks to the side, away from me, so I change direction, heading toward our table. It's in the middle of the room, the only one set up since I have claimed the entire restaurant for the night. Not a small feat and I owe Brax a bottle of Macallan 26 for arranging this.

There's a pause before I hear her follow me, a beat where I question my judgment before my smirk locks itself firmly in place. I guess I do still know my girl.

"I told you we weren't having dinner." She slides into the chair opposite me.

"And yet, here we are."

"Fine, you can feed me, but only because I'm exhausted from av—" A groan escapes from her full, pink lips, forming a small O shape. And just like that my semi grows to a fully-fledged hard-on.

"It was you." Her index finger points at me accusingly. "Oh my God, how did I not realize? You arranged this whole thing!"

I take a moment, because this is too good not to enjoy just a little bit, and pour us each a glass of water.

"No idea what you're talking about. This was just lucky timing." I raise my glass and gulp down some water, enjoying the way Wyatt's eyes watch me, glued to my mouth.

Giving herself a small shake, she reaches for the menu and slowly peruses it, purposefully ignoring me.

"The salmon is supposed to be good here."

Her nose scrunches up again, this time in disgust.

"I am not eating that. Christ, do you remember that time Charlie made those homemade salmon sushi rolls?"

"And the salmon was bad?" I laugh. "We spent the next twenty-four hours puking our guts up, that's not something you forget."

"I've never been able to look at salmon since then." She shudders. "She still lives off it though."

"Charlie always was a stickler for routine." I shrug.

"How did she ever put up with us?" Wyatt's shoulders bounce with a small chuckle.

"No idea," I respond, giving myself a silent pat on the back for my wicked distraction skills. "What happened with that sculpture you were telling me about last time? Did you hear back from the guy who was interested in commissioning it?"

"I did, he's wanting a little more time to decide, which suits me."

We're interrupted by a waiter and I give him my order, watching Wyatt out of the corner of my eye. She's flustered, a hand fluttering about her long neck, her fingers tracing the spot right behind her ear where I know a small tattoo of a bird in flight is hidden. My tongue used to take such pleasure in that spot.

"Uh, I'm sorry, I'm not sure, it all looks so good."

I smile, amused, as she anxiously tries to make a decision. One of her little quirks was that she always had to know what she was going to order before we ever went out for a meal. If she didn't get a chance to check out the menu beforehand, she would um and ah for far too long, unable to make a decision on the spot.

"Their parmesan risotto is supposed to be amazing," I nudge her, remembering how obsessed she was with anything cheesy.

"That does sound good." She throws me an appreciative look and hands the menu to the waiter. "I'll have that, please."

"So why are you glad the guy wants more time?" I question once we are on our own again.

"I haven't done any sculpting in a long time and it's going to be a difficult piece." She chews on her bottom lip. "If I'm honest, I'm probably not the right person for it, I've focused much more on painting the last few years. That's really where my heart is."

"Then why are you even considering taking the commission?"

"Money." She reaches across the table for her glass. "The book illustrations are a nice steady income, they gave me the freedom to quit working at the diner, but I'm not exactly rolling in cash. The commission would just give me a bit of breathing room."

My brow furrows. Money shouldn't be an issue for her. I've always sent her as much as I could every month. Despite the fact that we were never technically divorced, I made sure I took care of my financial responsibilities, sending her what I considered to be alimony every month.

"Wait, why do you need money?"

She looks startled at my tone and I try to reel it back in a bit, but I'm fucking confused.

"Well, being an artist doesn't always pay that great." She quirks an eyebrow at me. "For most of us anyway."

"I send you money, Wyatt. Every month." My hands clench the edge of the table.

"Oh, I don't touch that," she replies dismissively.

"Why the fuck not?"

"Because it's not mine." Her expression tells me she's confused by the direction this conversation has taken. "Why are you acting so pissed off?"

"Because I am pissed off," I bark. "What kind of man lives the life I'm living while his wife is struggling to get by?"

Wyatt glances around nervously. Pacified when she doesn't spot anyone within hearing range, she turns to me angrily.

"I am not your wife, and I don't need you to take care of me. Just because we never ended this legally, it doesn't change what happened. You left me."

"You didn't give me a choice."

"Wyatt? You home?" My voice echoes in the empty room. I dump my guitar on the empty armchair and flop down onto the sofa, scrubbing the heel of my hand over my painful eyes. The gig went well last night, but the four-hour drive home after was a killer. I didn't want to stay overnight in Shiner and away from Wyatt even longer than necessary. She seems to be doing better at the moment, but I like to be around, just in case.

Getting no response, I drag my ass to our tiny kitchen and take a drink of juice right from the carton before heading to our bedroom, ready to curl up next to my wife and get some sleep.

Doing my best to be quiet so I don't wake her, I pull up short when I spot the empty bed. Assuming she's gone out for a run, something her new therapist recommended she take up, I strip down to my boxers and slide under the covers. Stretching out to take advantage of having the bed to myself, my hand hits something hard shoved under Wyatt's pillow.

Pulling it out, I stare hard at the blue notebook. She's been scribbling away in this for months. Another technique her therapist suggested to help her cope, and one she's taken to much more easily than the running.

Sitting up, I balance the book on my knees and try to talk myself out of reading it. We've been so disconnected this past year, both of us lost in our own grief. I would do literally any-fucking-thing to make her better and to possibly have the answers right in my hands? There's no way I can resist that temptation.

Before I can change my mind, I open the book, my eyes quickly skimming the entries. Wyatt's normally perfect handwriting is messy and haphazard, making it difficult to read, but words jump out at me. Words that have me rubbing my chest, trying to ease the ache.

"What the fuck are you doing?"

You would think the sound of her voice—her obviously angry voice—would stop me, but my eyes continue to devour her pain and numbness begins to seep into the very fiber of my being.

I feel the bed dip beneath me but, still, I keep reading, until the book is viciously snatched away. Looking up, I take in her red face. Tiny drops of perspiration bead her hairline and her mouth is turned down in an aggressive frown.

Suddenly, the memory of the first time I ever saw her rushes at me. She was all big smiles and innocent happiness. She radiated unadulterated joy and, after surviving my parents' messy divorce and a cross-continent move, she was everything I wasn't. I have no idea what she ever saw in me, but I needed her from that very first minute. She was as necessary to me as oxygen, vital for my survival.

But this girl kneeling on the bed before me now with tears glistening? She's a broken version of my Cherry.

And I did that.

"You should have told me." I don't recognize my own voice.

"Told you what?" She shifts back and swings her legs, moving away from me. Always moving away from me.

"The truth."

She laughs, a small, ironic laugh that hurts more than any physical blow ever has.

"You want the truth, Flynn?" Her entire body stills by the bedroom door, her back to me. "Our baby is dead and it's because of you. Every time I look at you, I hate you a little more." Then she walks away.

❧

She slumps back in her seat, her shoulders sag and she looks exhausted.

"I'm sorry. What I said to you that day was—" She shakes her head, worrying her bottom lip. "It was cruel. So cruel."

"It was true." This isn't a conversation I want to have right now. "Anyway—"

"It's not true, Flynn. It's not." She leans forward, her face animated. "Please tell me you haven't believed that all these years?"

"It doesn't matter."

"Yes, it does. God," she whispers. "I'm so sorry."

I clear my throat, not knowing what to say. Which, I'm pretty sure is a first for me.

"Flynn." There's an urgency in her voice that draws my eyes back to her. "I never really hated you, or blamed you, or-or, I don't know! I was just so fucking angry, and it hurt so much, but if I focused on hating you then I didn't have to think about how much I wished I had died that night too." Her voice breaks off with a choked cry. "I wanted her so much, Flynn, and hating you hurt less than missing her. But I'm so sorry I pushed you away, because losing you?" Tears slide down her cheeks and she wipes them away, frustratedly. "Losing you as well, that broke me."

CHAPTER NINE

His eyes don't leave mine, the deep brown gaze as intense as ever.

"I thought leaving would let you move on." His face is tormented as though the thought of hurting me is causing him physical pain. "That if you didn't have to face the person responsible for what happened, you could stop reliving it."

I watch him closely, seeing the storm of emotion pulsing within him and, not for the first time, I consider how the last ten years have been for him.

Only this time, I don't presume to know the answer.

"What about you?" My voice is barely audible. "How did you get past it?"

"Music," he replies simply. "Music saved me when I had no interest in being saved."

A small smile plays across my lips. I remember distinctly how he would deal with any turmoil in his life. Locking himself away in a room with just his guitar, a pencil, and paper, playing and writing until he had worked through whatever issue was bothering him.

For the first time, I am envious of that passion.

I wish that I had been able to save him.

"I'm glad." I reach for my drink and run my fingertip around the rim. "I'm glad you got your dream, Irish. You deserve it."

There's a long pause and then he sighs. A bone-weary sigh from deep within his chest before he slumps back in his chair.

"I didn't get my dream, Wyatt. You were my dream."

&a;

"No, you're lying!"

"I swear to God."

"Ugh, I would have died!" I laugh.

The last few hours have flown by. Our earlier conversation was interrupted by the arrival of our food. Conveniently for Flynn, it was right after his declaration. He then promptly used the distraction as an opportunity to change the subject.

He always thought he was so stealthy, with some kind of ninja-like distraction skills. I want to roll my eyes just thinking about it. He never realized it only ever worked when I also wanted to change the subject.

I'm in dangerous territory here and I need to put a stop to this before it goes any further. Being with me will only ever cause Flynn unhappiness and, if there is one thing his reappearance in my life has reinforced, it's that I love him too much to be the cause of any more of his pain.

I also know him well enough to know that he is going to be hard enough to put off as it is. If he gets even a whiff of hesitance from me, he'll never give up.

"Yeah, well, I was more ready to kill than die, but whate—" The sound of his cell phone interrupts him and he grimaces when he checks the caller ID, before pressing ignore.

"Hey, Cherry?"

"Mmmm?"

"I think it's time we call it a night and you invite me back to your place for coffee."

I raise an eyebrow. "Coffee, huh?" The sight of his smirk, and more importantly how my core is clenching in response to it, sends me into a panic.

"Flynn." I sigh.

"Wyatt," he challenges.

"It's—" His phone jolts to life again, but he silences it without even a glance. "It's a bad idea."

"I think it's a fucking brilliant idea."

My face heats at his words and all I can do is hope that the dimmed lighting hides the effect. Before I can come up with an appropriate off-hand response, we are interrupted by the same girl from the reception desk.

"Excuse me, sir? I'm sorry to interrupt your meal, but you have an urgent phone call." She hands Flynn a portable handset, offers a discreet smile and exits as quietly as she entered.

Flynn glowers at the phone before he brings it to his ear and barks out, "What."

He listens for a moment, his forehead creasing and I'm struck by memories of stroking a hand over him, smoothing it across his brow, in an effort to remove those same creases. How many times did I do that over the years?

"Shit. Okay, yeah, send them in." The phone is slammed down on the table and he exhales a harsh breath. "A blogger posted that I was here and now there's a shitload of photographers out front."

He scowls at the table, lost in his own thoughts while I try to process this information. I don't know why this is a surprise. Once I had reached a place where his name inspired more happiness than regret, I vigilantly stalked him through social media, magazines, and television, anything I could, in a desperate attempt to stay connected to him in some small way. I cheered his successes and hurt over his—very rare—failures. So, it shouldn't come as any surprise that if I spend time with him, the paparazzi would find out. But for some reason it does. I feel rattled, and a sense of unease blankets me.

The double doors at the entrance of the restaurant are flung open and two hulking giants barrel their way in. After indulging in the tranquil atmosphere of Serenity by Havenworth today, with its unassuming staff, the dominating presence of these guys is disconcerting.

"Wyatt, this is Zane and Connor, my security guys." He pushes away from the table, standing abruptly and addressing the larger of the two. "I'll go out the front with Connor, you take Wyatt out the back. You arranged another car?"

The big guy, Zane? Nods. "Campbell organized it before he called you. Both cars should be waiting. I really think I should take yo—"

"You'll take Wyatt," he commands. "Do they know who I'm here with?"

Connor, I guess, moves closer to the table.

"No, Giselle only posted that you were spotted here having dinner. No mention of Miss Monroe."

"Giselle? I should've known."

My head, which has been bouncing between these three imposing men, stops on Flynn.

"Who is Giselle?" My question stings with accusation. Yeah, so Flynn wasn't the only one with jealousy issues, sue me.

For the first time since he took the call, Flynn's visage relaxes, and he lets loose with a low chuckle.

"Giselle Cross, she's an entertainment blogger. Think Perez Hilton, but bitchier."

"Oh. She sounds delightful," I respond drolly.

"Yeah, she's a fucking treasure." He takes hold of my hand and pulls me up, using slightly too much force so I fall into him, and have to place a hand on his chest to steady myself. The feel of his body pressed up against mine fires up every synapse, leaving me wanting.

Oh, he's good.

Never one to ignore an opportunity, he leans down, and his lips find mine. Slowly, so goddamn slowly, his mouth slides against mine before he takes a taste, his tongue gently tracing the line of my bottom lip. Then, without warning, he bites down and as his teeth sink into the fullness of my lip, a pulse throbs violently in my clit.

Pulling away, he places a final, gentle kiss on the spot behind my ear where my tattoo resides. The same spot that makes my eyes roll back in my head.

He nods toward Zane and my face flames, realizing what they just witnessed.

"You go with Zane and he'll take you back to your apartment. Connor and I will lose the photogs and then I'll come to you."

His words snap me back to reality and, as much as I wish things were different, it's important I make it clear that this is not going to go any further.

Ever.

"Don't do that." I make sure my voice is firm in an effort to undo any confusion that kiss caused. "Tonight was fun, but it's not going to happen again."

I hear the shuffle of feet behind me, an embarrassed clearing of a throat, but Flynn ignores it, keeping his stare fixed on me for an uncomfortable moment.

"Let's go, Connor. Zane, make sure no one follows you." Then he strides out without looking back.

I follow Zane through the kitchen, heading for the back entrance, eager to get home and put this night behind me. My emotions are too chaotic, and I need to get some distance.

The kitchen is almost empty at this late hour. Plus, I

assume with only two diners they were using a skeleton staff, so there is an awkward silence lingering as I do my best to keep up with Zane's fast pace.

"So, how long have you been working for Flynn?" My question is graceless with no subtlety, but after I walk through my door tonight this will all be over, so I make no apologies for trying to scam as much information as I can before then.

"Four years."

His voice is sharp and does not encourage discussion so, with a small sigh, I take the hint and focus on following him through the darkened corridor. When we finally reach the emergency exit, I take a deep breath before the door is pushed open and cross my fingers no paparazzi have made their way back here.

We step outside and I exhale gratefully when all I see is a black SUV idling by the curb, ready and waiting to get us out of here.

"This way, Miss Monroe." Zane places a hand on my back and guides me in the direction of the car. Just as he is about to open the door, a voice calls out to us, surprising me and sending Zane's hand diving for his belt.

"Oh, relax, Zane. It's just me."

I look up to see a gorgeous blonde with the most startling blue eyes. She's tall and willowy, beautiful in a quirky way, and she looks exceedingly out of place in this dingy alleyway. Her eyes are narrowed, shrewdly appraising me and I have the uncomfortable feeling that she finds me lacking.

Zane opens the door, encouraging me into the car,

but I can't seem to pull myself away from Giselle's scrutiny.

"You must be Wyatt Monroe."

I try to answer, but my voice catches in my throat.

"Interesting. Not what I expected." She tilts her head to the side, eyes wide and then flashes me a beautiful smile that transforms her entire face into something extraordinary. "Tell Flynn, he really needs to talk to his manager. I've made him an offer it's in his best interest to accept."

Before I can respond, Zane steps in front of me and gently pushes me into the car. We're in motion before I can react and, as we head in the direction of my apartment, all I'm left with are Giselle's words hanging over my head.

CHAPTER TEN

FLYNN

I flop down onto the seat of the town car, the smile that has been fixed to my face for the last twenty minutes while I dealt with the press, disappears as soon as the door closes behind me.

"Guys." I nod at Campbell and his husband, Simon. "Thanks for the ride."

"Don't worry about it," Campbell assures me.

I slump into the seat, beyond pissed about this interruption to my night.

Once Connor has taken his seat in the front, I tap my driver on the shoulder. "Chris, I need to go to Wyatt's."

He was the one who picked me up in the early hours a few weeks ago, so I know he has her address programmed in the navigation.

"No problem. It should only take twenty minutes."

"Thanks, man." I fall back against the leather, scrubbing a hand over my jaw.

It takes me a moment to notice the strange silence

in the car. You normally can't shut these guys up, but when I glance at them, they are sitting tersely, side by side and the air is thick with tension.

"You guys good? Did I interrupt something?"

"No, we're fine," Campbell rushes to answer.

Simon turns and glares at him. "You need to tell him."

That statement grabs my attention and I sit up a little straighter.

"Tell me what?" I look between the both of them, noticing how nervous Cam suddenly looks. "Tell me what, Campbell."

He removes his thick, black-framed glasses and rubs a knuckle across his brow.

"We have a little situation with Giselle Cross, but it's nothing to worry about, Flynn." He offers a small smile. "I'm taking care of it."

Simon shakes his head and turns to scowl out the window.

"Gotta say, I'm pretty fucking worried." Giselle is a nasty piece of trash. I made a mistake with her years ago and she's been determined to ruin my reputation ever since, portraying me as some kind of pussy-obsessed douche with anger management problems. She takes a tiny seed of truth and blows it up into the scandal of the decade over and over.

Anger creates a violent throb in my temple when a thought occurs to me.

"Does this involve Wyatt?"

Campbell slides his glasses back on and looks at me apologetically.

"She knows about the marriage. She's threatening to go public with it."

"Unless?" There's always an unless with people like her.

"Unless you agree to give her exclusive behind-the-scenes access on the upcoming tour."

"No fucking way." I shake my head angrily. "She thinks I'm going to let her tour with us? She's out of her fucking mind."

"Wait a minute, Flynn, think about it." He holds up a hand to stop my rant. "Think about Wyatt. Will she want her business splashed across every gossip magazine? We agree to this, and Giselle promises she can keep her sources quiet and she won't run with the story. Ever."

"So she says." I scoff. "You can't trust that bitch."

"Maybe, maybe not. But we can get a contract and threaten her with legal action if she ever breaks it." He sighs and looks at me resignedly. "Right now, we need to start damage control. I'll start divorce proceedings on Monday. An ex-wife is nowhere near as big a story as a secret wife. Considering you've been separated for so long, it should be pretty straightforward and I'm confident we can keep it quiet with some well-placed money."

That violent throb of anger I felt earlier multiplies in size as the words leave his mouth.

"I'm only going to say this once, so you need to listen very carefully," I seethe, my voice low and deadly. "I am not divorcing Wyatt. That is never going to happen."

Campbell blows out a breath of pure frustration.

"Fine, then I hope she's ready to have her life put on show for everyone to judge."

"You know what, Cam? Don't worry about my girl. She might not like it, but she can handle it. She can handle any shit they throw at her."

A loud groan of frustration reminds us both of Simon's presence.

"Hey, here's an idea. Just throwing this out there, but why don't you ask her what she thinks about all of this?"

The stairs creak under my feet as I climb the three flights to Wyatt's apartment. Once again, I notice the yellowing paint is peeling away on the walls and hand railings. While the building isn't decrepit by any stretch of the imagination, it is obviously old with an air of disrepair. All of which makes sense now that I know she has been refusing my money.

She always was fucking stubborn, determined to do things for herself with no help from anyone.

I finally reach her door and after noting that it's only nine o'clock, definitely not too late for a visit, but late enough that I might not actually be able to get this night back on track, I knock.

The low hum of the television that I had heard only moments before suddenly stops and I wait expectantly. When her footsteps never appear, I cock an eyebrow in disbelief.

"Really, Wyatt? This is how you're going to play it? Okay, then." I slide down on my ass, taking a seat by her door. "I've got all night."

I don't have to wait long before I hear her storming toward the door. She yanks it open and glares at me with an impressive scowl.

"You know, you used to listen better."

"Yeah, well you used to be braver, I guess we both changed some, huh."

Standing, I stretch quickly and move past her into the apartment before she can stop me.

But I do hear her whispered, "Asshole," as I walk by.

"We need to talk, Cherry." I flop down on the sofa, making myself at home. As I swing my legs up and recline back, I flash back to the last time I was on this couch and my cock twitches at the memory. I'll have to find a place for this when I finally get her moved in with me. Can't go throwing out happy memories like that.

"Jesus, make yourself at home, why don't you?" she grouses, taking a seat on the armchair opposite me, her legs curled under her ass.

I lick along my bottom lip as I recall the vivid memories I have of that ass reddening under the bite of my hand. Shit. I try to discreetly adjust myself and concentrate on something other than how good her pussy feels tightening around my cock when I'm buried deep inside her.

"So, I met Giselle Cross."

Her words have the same effect as a bucket of cold

water and I no longer have to worry about disguising my hardening cock.

"Of course, you fucking did." I'm pissed at myself for not realizing Wyatt was vulnerable when I didn't see Giselle out front of the spa. "What did she say?"

"Something about you talking to your manager about an offer she had made." She shrugs. "She knew my name."

I scrub a hand through my hair, my earlier annoyance back in full force.

"She knows about you. The marriage, I mean."

Her shoulders slump and she sags back in the seat.

"I was worried that's what it was about." She glances across at me, her eyes concerned. "Does she know about Carys?"

"No," I assure her, and she nods, her expression contemplative.

"What does this mean for you? Will it cause trouble for the album release?"

"Doesn't mean shit to me." I sit up and lean forward, my elbows on my knees. "It does mean you're about to be thrown to the wolves though. You gonna be okay with that?"

"It doesn't sound like I have much of a choice."

There is a note of regret in her voice that I loathe and the instinct to protect her kicks in.

"Yeah, you do." Her eyes brighten slightly, silently encouraging me to go on. "She says she won't post the story if I give her backstage access on the tour."

"She's bribing you?" Her voice vibrates with indignation.

"Don't sound so surprised, baby, those people will do anything to get a story."

"But it's so disgusting! What kind of person does that?"

"The shitty kind. But I'll do it if you want me to. Just say the word."

Her eyes narrow at me. "You are not giving her what she wants." Her face softens, and she continues. "You don't need to save me, Flynn. I can do that all by myself."

"I know you can," I agree because there's not a doubt in my mind that's true. "But that's what we do. We save each other."

She snorts out a laugh and pulls the collar of her sweatshirt over her mouth, mumbling something.

"I didn't catch any of that, try again."

She looks at me, her gaze contrite. "We've been doing a pretty crappy job of it."

"Fuck that. You've been saving me since the day I met you. We might have gotten lost along the way, but we're going to fix that." My voice is determined, challenging her to disagree with me.

She stands abruptly and begins pacing the small room.

"Flynn, you need to listen to me and actually hear what I'm saying." She moves to the sofa and sits down but stays far enough away to be out of reach. "You and I are not going to happen."

I unconsciously move toward her, the pull too much to resist.

"You and I already happened. We are happening." I

reach out and run a finger along her collarbone, relishing the goose bumps that chase my touch. "We will always be happening."

She jerks back, pulling away from me and shakes her head.

"We need to get a divorce." Her voice is soft, resigned, and she stands, making a concerted effort to distance herself from me. "We should've done it a long time ago. It was so stupid to think we would never have to deal with it." Once again, she moves closer to me and I don't think she even realizes she's doing it. But the push and pull is obvious to me.

"I can't afford a lawyer, but I trust you. If you get the papers drawn up, I'll sign them. I don't want anything, so it should be quick and painless."

When she's finished her bullshit rambling, I stand, slowly unfurling myself from the sofa and stalk toward her.

She must sense my aggravation because she begins to back away, a look of defiance on her face. When her back hits the wall, I lift my arms and cage her in. I lower my face, gliding my nose along hers, only stopping when my mouth is a breath away from her own.

"You think ending us would be painless?" I shake my head, bemused.

"We. Are. Not. Getting. Divorced." My lips ghost across hers and I have to stifle a smirk when a shiver runs through her. "Say it with me, Cherry."

It's possible I have taken it too far because as the words leave my mouth, her eyes, which were glazed over only seconds ago, clear now and she pushes me away.

"Yes, we are." She moves across the room and pulls the door open aggressively. "Now, you need to leave."

"We need to talk about what's going to happen. You're not prepared to deal with the press."

She shrugs her shoulder petulantly and levels me with a cold glare.

"Lots of crazy people shoving cameras in my face and screaming questions at me. Nothing you say is going to prepare me for that. Now, go."

There's no point in me standing here arguing with her, not when she's like this, so I walk toward the door, doing my best to keep my face indifferent.

I walk past her and just as I hear the door start to close behind me, I stop.

"Wyatt?"

"Ugh, what?"

"We're really not, though."

CHAPTER ELEVEN

"Oh my God, that was insane." Layla's sweet voice is filled with disbelief as she slides onto a barstool at my kitchen counter. "There are about twenty photographers out there! Now I understand why you didn't want to go out."

"Yeah, it only took them a day or two to find my home address after the story broke. They've been parked out there ever since." I slide a mug of steaming peppermint tea in front of her, which she accepts gratefully.

I've been doing my best to keep my stress levels, as well as my temper, under control these last few weeks, but it's been difficult. Having my photo splashed all over the internet has been awful and, while I'm grateful they haven't discovered the truth about the end of our relationship, I'm not thrilled with the narrative they're creating. If social media is to be believed, we were young, dumb kids playing at being grown-ups, until

Flynn came to his senses and left to pursue his dream of fame in LA.

Depending on who you talk to, either Flynn's the asshole who broke his first loves heart or I'm a first-class bitch who tried to stop him from achieving his dreams.

Cue eye roll.

"This is actually a quiet day. Normally there's about fifty of them, but most took off a few hours ago." I quirk an eyebrow and grin. "I guess a real celebrity is getting into some kind of trouble."

"How are you coping with all of this? What does Flynn say?" She blows on the tea and takes a cautious sip.

"It's driving me crazy." I groan. "I haven't left the apartment in days because I thought if they weren't getting anything from me, they would leave, but nope. He just says to ignore them and say nothing. It's getting harder to do, though."

"That sounds like a nightmare," she agrees before lowering her voice to a whisper. "I still can't believe you're married. Married!"

"I know, I suck. I swear I am well and truly aware of my level of friendship suckiness."

"No, I mean I get it." She reaches across the break-fast bar and gives my hand a gentle squeeze. "I defi-nitely understand where you're coming from, wanting to put that behind you. I guess I understand better now why you wanted me to be absolutely sure before I gave up on Ethan. I will never be able to thank you enough for that. If I hadn't fought for him." She shakes her head, her eyes tearing up. "It would have been the biggest mistake of my life."

"Hey, but you did listen. At least someone learned from my mistakes." I force a laugh and hope I'm pulling off this whole nonchalant thing.

"You know, Cassidy told me once that you really helped her get her head straight about Mason too. Perhaps it's time you take your own advice since it's always the grade-A, top-notch stuff."

This time my laugh is far from forced, slipping out easily.

"I'll remind you of that next time you ignore my advice!"

"That has never happened, don't even try it." Layla chuckles before sobering. "You don't think you and Flynn could try again?"

"I don't want to try again." I force down the bile from my lie.

"Okay, but does he know that? CJ said he's refusing a divorce."

"Yeah, he's being an ass about that, but he's been amazing through everything else, so I don't want to push my luck. I'll probably end up filing myself."

"Amazing, how?" Layla's eyes light up mischievously with her question, but I choose to ignore it.

"Just talking me through it, I guess. He calls every day to keep me updated with how his team is trying to contain the story, that sort of thing. Plus, he gave me some security so I don't have to deal with the paps by myself. I think the best thing, for us anyway." I straighten up from the counter, my hands wrapped around my coffee mug. "Is that he can't come here. I think a bit of distance will help him get over this idea that we're going to get back together. He's back in the city and I'm sure if it wasn't for those idiots outside, he would be here trying to wear me down."

"Well, I mean, that's kind of sweet though, yeah? He must really love you." She sighs sadly. "I wish you felt the same, you deserve a happily ever after."

I force a bright smile and ignore the painful knot in my gut.

"I have my happily ever after, Lay. It just doesn't involve a man. Anyway." I shake off the gloom. "I'm so sick of talking about me, what about you? How are the wedding plans coming?"

A beautiful smile briefly dances across Layla's lips before she sobers and looks down at her hands tightening around the mug, worrying her bottom lip with her teeth.

"Good, they're going good. We have decided to postpone the wedding a little bit though."

Okay, I did not see that coming.

I lean forward and take her hands in mine. I know I must look concerned because she immediately backtracks.

"Oh no, it's not anything bad, it's good news actually. Really good news." She pauses, and her warm brown eyes meet mine and I know. I just fucking know what she's about to say.

"I'm pregnant."

"Right." The word escapes on an exhale.

"I wanted to tell you first, by ourselves." She rushes

on, her concern written all over her face. "Are you okay?"

Am I okay? There's no simple answer to that. I'm terrified I will never be okay.

Instead, I slip on my mask and I tell her what she needs to hear.

"Of course, I am. Lay! God, I'm so excited for you both."

"Really?" She physically slumps down in relief. "Because it's okay if you're not, you know. I would completely understand."

"Sweetie, what happened to me was a long time ago, I'm fine. Please don't worry about me."

"Okay, if you're sure?" She eyes me tentatively.

My head is screaming at me, my body desperate to collapse into itself, and in this moment, I hate myself a little. Because the sweetest girl in the world is standing in front of me and she would be devastated if she knew what her news was doing to me. So, I hold it together and move around the breakfast bar and wrap her up in a giant hug.

"I'm sure," I whisper.

An hour later, I close the door behind Layla and turn my back to it, slowly sliding down until my ass hits the ground.

The last hour proved to be endless as I listened to excited chatter and fearful musings, all the while fighting for control of my emotions. Layla tried so hard to hold back, her concern for me evident but there was no disguising her joy.

My head sinks to my knees and my chest tightens painfully. I don't understand why this hurts so much more than when Skye and Cassidy told me they were pregnant, but this pain feels raw and intense in a way it didn't then. Like my heart is a gaping open wound and I'm prodding it with a sharpened fingernail in an effort to see how much agony I can tolerate.

My breathing becomes labored as memories assault me. The could have beens. The should have beens. Most painful of all are the never will bes.

Grasping my chest, I begin to panic as my tears fall, causing my breaths to become even more ragged. The act of dragging air into my lungs seems too damn hard and my sobs grow harder, harsher, my throat closing in.

My phone goes off in my pocket and my first instinct is to ignore it, but fear and self-preservation has me answering it. I put the cell to my ear, but unable to speak, whoever is calling just gets an earful of me hyperventilating.

"Wyatt?"

Shit. Of course, it would be him.

"Wyatt, what's going on, are you okay?"

I try to answer him, tell him everything is fine, but I can't force the words out. Instead, my cries get louder, my breathing more forced.

"Relax, baby, I'm coming. I'll be there soon."

Common sense is shrieking at me to tell him to

stop, to stay away, but when he disconnects the call, all I feel is relief.

My breathing has leveled out, breaths coming easier by the time he hammers on my door. But the tears are still falling and no matter how many times I scrub my hands over my face to wipe them away, they keep on coming.

"Wyatt?" The banging continues. "Wyatt!"

Summoning every ounce of energy I have, I pull myself up and open the door.

"Jesus." Flynn takes one look at me and pulls me to him, wrapping his strong arms around me and holding tight.

All I can do is burrow my head into his chest and cry. I shed all the tears I should have cried ten years ago and then, all the tears I should have cried three years later when my life, once again, crashed down around me.

We stand there, for I don't know how long, me locked into his embrace, his mouth at my ear, reassuring me that I am going to be okay.

But he doesn't know. He doesn't know that I don't get to be okay.

That I can never be okay again.

Finally, I push away, putting some much-needed space between us.

"I'm sorry," I rasp out. "I'm fine, you didn't need to come over. You caught me at a bad moment."

He follows me deeper into the apartment and then stands still, watching me intensely as I move to the bathroom and wash my face with cold water.

I take a fortifying breath and then walk back toward him, attempting to project a hell of a lot more confidence than I'm feeling right now.

"You have many bad moments like that?" he questions with a raised brow, and I don't know why, but I feel judged.

"You've never had a bad day? Christ, Flynn, I just needed to cry it out. Nobody asked you to come rushing over like some kind of fucking white knight." I prowl around the room, unable to keep still, and I feel his eyes on me with every step I take.

"Fair enough. Do you want to talk about whatever it is that you needed to cry out?" His voice is gentle, and it strikes me that this is the Flynn who was by my side in the days, weeks, and months after we lost our baby girl.

It makes me want to lash out. It's not fair and it's not okay, but I want to hurt him. Because he still gets to have that one day.

He'll meet the woman he's destined for and they'll create the life that was supposed to be mine. A life with love and babies, art and music.

He'll be happy and while any other day I would tell you that's what I want for him, right now I want him to feel a tiny fraction of the misery I have to live with.

"Let's see, do I want to talk about the fact that one of my best friends is having a baby? Hmmm." I tap a finger on my chin in an exaggerated gesture. "Ya know what? No, I don't, but thanks for asking."

"Ah, fuck." He moves toward me, but I sidestep him and move to the kitchen. I feel him follow me, watching as I pull a bottle of vodka out of the refrigerator and grab a glass from the sink.

"It's okay to be angry, no one would blame you."

"Well, gee, thanks for that insight." I slam the drink down, enjoying the burn of the straight alcohol.

I storm back past him and suddenly all I can think about is getting out of this apartment. But of course, I can't. Because of him.

I turn around and face him. "I want you to go. Leave, now."

He leans back against the wall, not even slightly conflicted.

"I'm not going anywhere, Cherry."

"Yes, you are. Now!" I raise a hand and point to the door somewhat hysterically.

He pushes himself off the wall, frustration rolling off him in waves.

"Talk to me!" he yells. "If anyone understands this, it's me, so talk. To. Me."

"You think you understand?" I snort out an ironic laugh. "You don't understand shit."

"I lost her too, Wyatt." His voice is low and gravelly, full of pain. "You don't have a monopoly on grief. I have to live with it too."

I close my eyes and shake my head emphatically, tears biting behind my eyelids.

"It's not the same," I scream, losing all pretense of

control. "You can have another baby. You can have a hundred babies if you want." I point a finger at him aggressively. "So don't tell me you understand. You understand nothing."

"Wyatt." His voice calm and he walks purposefully toward me, his hands landing on my upper arms and squeezing gently. "You will too. We'll get our family. It might take us longer than we thought it would all those years ago, but you will hold our baby in your arms one day."

His words are meant to comfort me, but instead they steal the fight from me and I sag into his arms in defeat.

"No, I won't," I whisper. "Because I can't have children anymore."

CHAPTER TWELVE

FLYNN

Her face crumples slightly as the words leave her mouth, but she stares at me defiantly.

"What?" I need her to repeat herself because there's no way I heard what I think I just heard.

"I can't have kids, Flynn. So now you see why we will never work." She moves away from me, in the direction of the door. "You should go now, please."

I shake my head, walking in the opposite direction, and I take a seat at the small dinette set.

"I don't understand. The doctors never said you couldn't have kids." My mind is refusing to accept this. I was there. I was at every appointment. Every exam. We were warned that any future pregnancy would be high risk, but never, not once, did they say we couldn't have a baby.

Her shoulders drop, and she walks slowly over to the table, taking a seat opposite me. Her eyes are so fucking sad I have to look away.

"It happened a few years later. I was having horrible

117

abdominal pain and when I went to the doctor, I was diagnosed with endometriosis. More tests showed that I had severe scarring on both fallopian tubes." Her entire demeanor is resigned. "The chances of me getting pregnant are almost zero."

I can't look at her. Her pain is too much for me, so I keep my eyes locked on the huge picture window on the other side of the room and concentrate on keeping my breathing even.

"I warned you," she whispers, her voice aching with grief. "I told you we couldn't happen, I wish you'd just left it alone."

Her admission snaps me out of my trance and for the first time, I feel a surge of anger toward her.

"You think we won't be together because you can't have kids?"

"You want kids, Flynn. God, when I was pregnant, you were already talking about the next one." She leans forward and rests her head in her hands before continuing, her voice slightly muffled. "I can't give you what you want anymore."

I act instinctively, my hand slamming painfully down on the table.

"You are what I want. Don't you dare act like you're doing this for me." I fume. "You don't get to break my fucking heart again and tell me it's all for me."

"It is for you," she screams, shooting up. The sound of her chair crashing to the floor reverberates throughout the room. "I'm broken, Flynn, and do you know why I'm broken? Because I fucking ran toward a fire instead of away from it." Her voice cracks on a sob.

"What kind of fucking idiot does that, huh? I lost everything because I made one wrong decision. All of this"—she waves a hand between us—"is my fault. Mine."

She sinks to the ground, her hands covering her face and her body convulsing as tears slide down her face.

It's a moment before I can move, her words paralyzing me, but when I do, I can't get to her fast enough.

I wrap my hand around her neck and pull her to me, her cheek soft against my own. She clings on to my t-shirt, pulling me to her as though she is trying to climb inside me. I wish to God I had the words she needs, the words that can heal her. But all I can do is hold her and make promise after promise that we are going to survive this.

So that's what I do.

I hold her until her body calms and her pained wails taper down to quiet whimpers.

I hold her until her face turns to mine, her eyes troubled and her mouth swollen.

I hold her until her hands land on my jaw and the sound of her fingertips scraping along my stubble is all I can hear.

I hold her until our pain and need become entangled, charging the air around us.

Only when her lips find my neck do I let go. But just long enough to stand.

I drag her body up with me before my hands slide down along her curves and grasp her ass. Any illusion of control vanishes, and I slam my mouth to hers, all skill I have deserting me. It's messy and it's real. Just like us.

She moves against me, pushing me back, her mouth never breaking our connection. I take the hint and lower my grip to her thighs, curling around them and lifting her up. She wraps her legs around me, crossing her feet at my back, and grinding her pussy against the waistband of my jeans.

I turn and move quickly to her bedroom. Our bodies are connected from head to foot, but it's still not enough. The need to consume her, to wreck her once and for all for anyone else, fuels my movements.

She moans around my tongue and my cock hardens to the point of pain. I want to take my time with her, cherish her the way a real fucking man should, but neither one of us has the patience for that now.

I step blindly into her room, darkness enveloping us. Our bodies are movement and music, shadowed by melancholy, but driven by hope.

The last few steps to her bed are filled with urgent touches, her tongue sliding along mine with demanding strokes. I swallow her moans eagerly, the desire to taste her everywhere is devastating.

She bounces lightly when I drop her on the bed and a giggle falls from her lips that are now red and swollen and will look pretty fucking spectacular when they're wrapped around my cock later.

"Flynn?" The sound of her voice, small and unsure, distracts me, drawing my gaze up until I meet her eyes. "You gonna write a song about me one day?"

My heart thumps in my chest, racing in a way that makes me want to live forever just so I can experience it a million fucking times over.

The curve of Wyatt's breast is pressed against my chest, and I revel in her softness, the way she feels under me. Over me. Any fucking way I can get her.

This feeling is slightly unsettling, but far from unwelcome. I fucked a lot of girls back home, but none ever consumed me the way Wyatt Monroe has since the moment I saw her.

Her hand is playing across my stomach, her fingers teasing patterns along my skin and when a soft sigh slips out, her breath warms my chest.

She pulls back, turning slightly so she is facing me, and her eyes are assessing.

"I liked that."

A loud laugh rolls through me and not for the first time I consider how much I love her honesty.

"I liked it too." I chuckle, punctuating my words with a kiss to her nose.

"You gonna write a song about me one day?"

I shake my head at her question because she has no. Fucking. Idea.

Rolling over, I press my body up along hers and thread a hand through her hair, pulling her mouth to me. She tastes like cherry Chapstick and I can't get enough.

I pull back slightly, only a fraction of space between us, the heat of her breaths comforting, and I give her the only answer I have.

"Every song until the day I die."

&

I can't take my eyes off her, this moment shining a light on the vulnerability she normally hides so fiercely. Regret punches me in the gut as I realize exactly what I lost all of those years ago. I let guilt steal what I loved the most. I let it feed my demons and fuel my night-mares. Only she can heal me.

We can finally heal each other.

She watches me closely, exposed and waiting.

"Every song until the day I die."

Her smile is explosive, the pull between us proving too much for her to fight.

"Cherry?" There's an edge to my voice as I reach behind me and pull off my t-shirt.

"Hmmm." Her voice is perfectly distracted, her eyes locked on my hands that are now working my zipper down.

"Get your damn clothes off."

She balks at my demand, her eyes narrowing, a glint of defiance shining bright. Her mouth opens, probably to curse me out, but it closes just as quickly when I step out of my jeans and fist my cock roughly.

"Now."

She hops to her knees, teeth biting down on her bottom lip in a way that has me desperate to lick the sting away with my tongue. She makes quick work of removing her simple white tank and yoga pants leaving her incredible curves in black lace that I'm tempted to rip off.

"Turn around." There's a moment where I think she's going to argue with me, but instead her face softens and her eyes heat.

"You've gotten bossier, you know that?"

"I've just learned that sometimes you have to take what you want. Now, turn around."

This time there is no hesitation in her movement. She swings around and falls onto her hands and knees, ass up in the air just begging for my mouth.

I move toward her, my hand slowing on my cock before I remove it completely and glide it down her back. Slowly, following the curve of her spine, my hand splays out over her waist, spanning almost the entire distance. I press down, forcing her upper body down to the soft mattress and a harsh grunt pushes past my lips at the sight of her looking at me over her shoulder, her mouth open in a soft O.

Unable to hold back any longer, I step forward and slide her panties over her ass and down her thighs. I give her ass a fast, sharp slap and then slide my hand down, two fingers slipping easily through her pussy.

Her groan is muffled by the sheets and it causes my dick to pulse against her thigh.

"You want my mouth on you, Cherry?" I goad, a fingertip circling her already swollen clit. "You want me to take a little taste? Fuck you with my tongue first?"

Her eyes close and she pushes back against my hand.

"Less talking, more doing." She groans.

I smirk at the sound of her desperation and climb onto the bed. Pushing my aching cock into the mattress, I spread her legs as wide as her panties allow and swipe my tongue along her cunt. My first taste results in a full-body tremor from Wyatt and a strangled whimper that has me ready to come from that one sound alone.

My tongue plays with her clit until I can't take her sounds anymore, the need to get inside her too much. I stop playing around and start eating her out with the urgency of a desperate man. I use my tongue, my fingers, my teeth, loving the grind of her pussy against my face.

When I feel her clenching around my fingers, and my ears are ringing with the sound of her breathless stutters, I raise my face to her ass and bite down on her rounded cheek.

Wyatt falls limply to the bed, completely sated, her breathing harsh and I kneel behind her, a lewd smirk on my face.

"Don't wimp out on me just yet, baby. I'm not done with you."

I reach down and get a firm grip on her hips before I turn her over so she's on her back, pussy glistening and her hands making their way to her tits. Which are still, unfortunately, encased in the black lace I was getting a hard-on for, only moments ago.

Leaning down, I hover over her. My mouth ghosts along her lace-covered nipples, my heated breath sending a shiver of anticipation through her body. I lower my lips, running them over the pebbled tip, teasing her and enjoying the groan of frustration that hisses from between her teeth.

"I swear to God, if you don't put your mouth on me in the next three seconds, I will never blow you again." She lifts her head so she can meet my eye. "Ever."

I love it when she plays dirty.

I latch my mouth onto her nipple, sucking hard and enjoying the way her back arches off the bed, before biting down.

Kneeling back, I take a moment to savor the sight of her before moving down her body and placing a quick kiss on her cunt. Then I straighten and take my cock in hand, gently tapping it on her clit while I watch her watching us, her eyes locked on my dick sliding through her juices.

I ease the tip in, loving the stretch of her as she takes me, and when her hands grab at my ass trying to draw me in deeper, I give up any pretense of control and thrust in, fully seating myself.

Refusing to move just yet, I lower my mouth to her neck, kissing along the curve and enjoying the delicacy of her skin. My hands claim her; my touch marking her as mine.

She is pushing up against me, raising her hips in an effort to get some kind of friction, but I need something from her first.

"You want me to move?" I whisper, my mouth by her ear. I roll my hips just once.

"Yes. Please."

"We've got some stuff we need to work out first."

"Now?" Her voice is indignant and her face creases in frustration as she digs her hands into my ass harder.

"Well, I figure I have your full attention, I should probably take advantage." I pull back until just the tip of my cock is inside her and she groans out in annoyance.

"Fine."

"Good." I press my hips forward, pushing back into her roughly and she pushes her head back into the pillow. "You and I are married, yes?"

"Yes," she grits out.

I ease back out.

"And we are going to stay married. Yes?"

Her eyes flick to mine and she looks torn, her teeth worrying her bottom lip.

"Yes," she whispers.

I lower my forehead until it rests against hers and just feel her for a moment. The rise and fall of her chest. The slip of her hips against mine.

"Every song until the day I die," I rasp out before I slam home, thrusting into her, the need to come almost painful. My mouth takes hers in a savage kiss and when I feel her tightening around me, there is only one word echoing in my mind.

Mine.

CHAPTER THIRTEEN

A tendril of hair tickles my shoulder, fanning across every time Flynn exhales. My mind is struggling to catch up with everything that has happened over the last few hours.

My response to Layla's news was… overwhelming and unexpected. I knew her inevitable announcement would hurt. Seeing anyone pregnant, or with their children, is always a painful reminder. But it's usually tempered with happiness. Seeing the people I love truly joyful, makes my own sadness bearable.

But this devastation was paralyzing, and I can only put it down to the re-emergence of Flynn, and the chaos he has thrown my life into. I seem to be feeling everything so much more intensely, and for someone used to burying their feelings, it is proving to be a difficult transition for me.

Not to mention Flynn.

Ugh, *Flynn.*

Stubborn, won't-take-no-for-an-answer, asshole Flynn.

The look in his eyes when he was moving inside of me, telling me what our future holds, was extraordinary. Heat and determination mixed with love and reverence.

No one has ever looked at me like that, before or after him, and I want to experience it again. I want to be his again, and for him to belong to me, in every sense of the word. But I'm so scared he doesn't realize what committing to me again means. Everything he will have to sacrifice.

What if he wakes up one day and decides that I wasn't worth it.

"You about done overanalyzing everything?"

I startle at the sound of his husky whisper, freezing for a moment before I give in to the urge to relax my body into his.

He kisses my neck softly. Such a stark contrast to the way he was touching me only hours ago.

"Stop thinking about it." His hand slides up along my rib cage, cups my breast and gently squeezes my nipple, sending a jolt right to my core. "There's nothing *to* think about. There's nothing to do. We're good."

I push my ass back a little, grinding against his hardening cock.

"We are so far from good, it's laughable. But it's cute that you think so," I reply with a laugh.

He moves away from me briefly, putting unwanted space between our bodies before he uses a firm hand on my stomach to push me on my back. Then he moves over me, settling between my open legs, and we are chest to chest, nose to nose.

"I'm moving to the city. I'd prefer we lived somewhere with a bit more security, but if you want to stay here, we will." He rocks against me and his lips take a quick taste. "You can travel with me." His cock slides along my seam deliciously teasing me. "Or not. In which case I'll cut back on my touring."

A groan slips out when the tip of his dick makes contact with my pulsing clit, but I force myself to stay on task.

"You need to think about what you'll be giving up. It's not as straightforward as you're making it out to be."

"I'm not giving up shit. There are plenty of ways we ca—" He is cut off by the sound of pounding on the door.

"Wyatt!" More banging. "Wyatt! I just fought my way through a pack of swarming vultures to get in here, so open the motherloving door!"

Flynn's eyebrows shoot up. "Pink?"

"Cassidy." I giggle. "But, yes." I begrudgingly climb out from under him, looking for my clothes.

"Get dressed. She already thinks you have a giant dick, we don't need to confirm her suspicions."

He laughs loudly, and I relish the sound.

"Wyatt? Is someone in there with you?" Cass starts up her banging again. "Is it the rock star Romeo? *Let me in, Red!*"

Throwing on my yoga pants and tank top, sans bra and panties, I rush out of the room, closing the door behind me.

"I'm coming! Jesus Christ, Cass, calm yourself."

As soon as I open the door, she pulls me to her, wrapping me up in a giant bear hug.

"I'm so sorry it took me so long to get here. I had to track down my mom so she could take the kids."

She breaks the hug and pulls back. Her hands are holding mine and she looks at me with an assessing gaze.

"You look okay." I'm slightly put out that she sounds disappointed.

"I am okay. Now, why are you here?"

"Layla called me." She pushes past me and dumps her purse on the kitchen counter. "Why did it take you so long to answer the door?" She narrows her eyes at me.

"I was in bed." I cross my hands over my chest defensively.

"Bed? At"—her eyes shoot to the clock—"four in the afternoon?"

"I was tired. Do you want a drink? I'm all out of vodka, maybe you could run to the store and grab some?" Perfect. I can get Flynn out of here while she's doing that, and she never needs to know he was here.

Wait, why am I trying to hide him? If we're doing this, she's going to find out. Ugh, why am I so bad at this.

"I thought I heard a man laughing." Yep, there's that

single-eyebrow-quirking thing. "And, no, I don't want a drink. Are you trying to get rid of me?"

"Of course, she is." Flynn comes sauntering out of my room, looking all sex-disheveled and wearing a smirk. "How else can she sneak me out?"

"Ah." Cassidy's eyes light up. "It *was* Romeo. Nice to see you again."

"Romeo? Can I object to that nickname? It's really not working for me."

"Nope, it's pretty much set in stone now."

My eyes bounce between the two as they banter easily with each other.

"Then I guess I'm sticking with Pink for you." He shrugs carelessly.

"No." Cassidy is adamant.

"I call *her* Red." She nods to me. "So, you see, the whole hair-color-nickname thing is already played out."

"No." Flynn is equally adamant. "*She's* Cherry." He pulls me to him so my back is resting against his front, and I try to figure out what the ever-loving hell is going on here.

"Well, isn't this just a giant nickname clusterfuck," I state, incredulously. "How about we just stick to Flynn, Cassidy, and Wyatt, hmm?"

"How about we don't be such a Debbie Downer, hmmm?" she retorts before grabbing Flynn's hand and dragging him out from behind me.

"Come, Romeo. We have much to discuss."

❧

"So, you'll move then?"

"Yeah, I've already started looking at places. But it depends if she wants to move. Otherwise, we'll just stay here."

"Oh, she'll move. She's been talking about finding somewhere bigger for the last two years."

I sit on the armchair, legs crossed and nursing a warm-ish cup of coffee, feeling like I'm in some kind of weird alternative universe.

Cassidy and Flynn sit on opposite ends of the sofa, their bodies turned toward each other as they discuss the future of our relationship, apparently.

"I'm right here, you know." I wish I could tell you it didn't come out as petulantly as it sounded, but that would be a lie.

"Yes," Cassidy begins as if she's talking to her three-year-old twins. "But, as it turns out, you are notoriously bad at making good life choices, so Aunty Cass is here to help." She places a hand over her heart. "Out of love."

I roll my eyes. "You're ridiculous."

Flynn watches us with amused eyes before they dim suddenly. "She's a lot more eager to talk about our future than you are."

My heart does a little dive at the unabashed sadness on his face.

"I have a lot to make up for, but I want to start. Right fucking now, but you have to be prepared to let me." He sighs. "As much as I want to just tell you what's going to happen, we both know that wouldn't fly. So, you gonna do this with me?"

I consider what he's said. It's going to be hard. We both have so much guilt over Carys, even if, on my good days, I know that no one is to blame. That's going to challenge our relationship.

His life gets played out on the public stage and there's nothing that can prepare me for how hard that is going to be. That will definitely challenge us.

We're going to have to change the vision for our future. Because the future we saw when we took our vows all those years ago, is most likely never going to happen. No matter what he thinks, that will be a challenge.

If we choose to do this, there will be an inordinate amount of difficult times ahead of us.

But, despite all of that, I know that I haven't felt this alive since the day I walked out on him ten years ago. It feels good to *feel* again, and I know that we are up to every challenge we'll face. As long as we face them together.

"Yeah." I nod. "We're going to do it."

A slow, lazy grin makes its way across his face and my heart falters slightly at the sight.

He abruptly stands, his coffee cup falling to the side and the mocha liquid splashing all over the feather-gray fabric. In two short strides, he is standing in front of me, then pulling me up so that my body is flush against his.

"Fuck, yeah, we are." Then his mouth finds mine in a kiss that is as overwhelming as it is perfect.

"You guu-uys!" We're ripped from our moment by the sight of Cassidy gazing at us, her hands clutched in front of her heart and a wide grin on her face. "So, when are we going house hunting?"

CHAPTER FOURTEEN

FLYNN

"**J**esus Christ, why am I doing this again?" My muscles are straining under the weight of a huge handcrafted dresser that we are carrying through the lobby.

Said lobby being in the multimillion-dollar luxury building where our new home resides. Also, the lobby that currently has about ten residents watching us in disbelief, as if they have never seen someone actually move their own furniture.

"Because you love me," Wyatt calls from behind with a carefree laugh.

"I love you enough to hire the very best movers," I grit out. "So, that doesn't explain shit."

"You know I couldn't trust my grandma's dresser with movers," she chastises.

"Stop complaining like a little bitch, Romeo."

Yeah, so apparently Cassidy is a permanent fixture in my life now.

Can you say lucky?

"You know, Crazy, you're more than welcome to get your ass over here and help."

I look up and make eye contact with Mason, Cassidy's husband. The man has balls of steel, which is a good thing because he needs them to be married to her.

"Nobody asked you, Sunshine, but thanks for contributing." She blows him a kiss and he shakes his head in amusement. "Now, will you two hurry up, I ordered a pizza and it would be just awesome if you could have this set up before it gets here."

Wyatt rushes past and places a kiss on my jaw. "I'll make this up to you tonight, I promise."

We spend the next twenty minutes navigating this ridiculously huge piece of furniture through the lobby and up the service elevator.

"Right, where do you want it?" Mason and I are standing in the doorway to the bedroom. There really is only a few places it could go, so I'm expecting a quick response. Instead my question is met with first silence, and then some muttered umms and aahs.

"Mason?" I look at the equally frustrated man opposite me. "You want a beer?"

"Fuck, yeah."

We drop the dresser right where we're standing and make our way to the kitchen, leaving the outraged cries of the girls behind us.

I stand in front of the giant SubZero refrigerator that is far too big for just Wyatt and me, and pull out a couple of beers, handing one to Mason. "Hey, man, thanks for the tip on this place." I lean against the granite counter. "We were having trouble finding somewhere, so it was a godsend."

He nods his head in acknowledgment and rubs a hand across his jaw. "Yeah, it can be a bitch to find something decent, especially here. I'm dreading having to start looking for somewhere new."

"You guys are moving?"

"We're thinking about it. There's a culinary school in Paris that Cassidy would love to go to and we figure it would be great for the kids, so we'll see."

"What?"

Mason and I look over to see Wyatt and Cassidy standing on the step leading up to the raised kitchen. Wyatt looks horrified and Cassidy looks ready to kill.

"You're moving to Paris?" Wyatt turns to Cassidy, eyes wide.

"No." She scoffs and strides determinedly toward Mason. "I am going to kill you," she whispers loudly.

"Why wouldn't you tell us that?" Wyatt follows her and takes a spot beside me. Leaning into me, her hand settles on my stomach, a little too close to the waistband of my jeans for my comfort.

"There's nothing to tell, it's just something we were talking about." She waves us off. "Like, wouldn't it be great if unicorns were real or wouldn't it be awesome if I could have multiple orgasms every time. It's nice to think about, but it's never going to *actually* happen."

"It could happen, though, if you weren't such a stubborn ass," Mason insists, taking a long pull of his beer.

"Not getting multiple orgasms has nothing to do with my ass, Sunshine."

"Cass," Wyatt interjects and thank fuck for that. "That sounds like an incredible opportunity, why wouldn't you do it? I mean it would suck for us, we would miss you so much, but think about everything you could learn over there."

Cassidy pushes away from the counter and heads to the refrigerator.

"I'm not saying it will never happen, just not right now." She opens the door and examines the empty shelves, before turning to me with a quirked brow. "You know, considering you're a millionaire rock star I would have thought you'd have something to feed your guests."

Mason folds his arms across his chest, his eyes narrowed.

"Now is the perfect time to do this. The kids are young, we have enough in savings to live over there for a few years and if worse came to worst, I can pick up some freelance consulting work if I need to," he argues. "You're making excuses, Crazy."

She slams the door shut and Wyatt and I exchange an awkward look. Watching our friends have a knock-down, drag-out fight isn't the way I saw this night ending.

"Really? You really want to give up your job at the Youth Center and go back to corporate work? *That's* what you want?" she challenges.

"It might not even be necessary, but if I had to, I would. It wouldn't be forever, and the benefits would far outweigh the negatives."

"Ugh, would you stop being so damn logical, it's annoying as fuck."

Wyatt moves away from me and wraps Cassidy in a hug, whispering something in her ear. She rolls her eyes in response but pulls Wyatt to her tightly.

"We'll talk about it at home," she tells Mason over Wyatt's shoulder. "I promise."

The moment is interrupted by the buzz of the concierge phone by the front door and I move for it, eager to make an escape from the tension in the room. Probably an asshole move to leave it for Wyatt to deal with, but let's face it, out of the two of us she's the most likely to actually help.

"Yeah."

"Good evening, Mr. Maguire. This is Eleanor from concierge. I'm sorry to bother you but you have a pizza delivery here for you and they are refusing to leave the order with me."

"No problem, I'll be right down."

Three minutes later I walk into the lobby and find myself coming to a complete standstill when I see who is waiting there holding our pizza.

Giselle fucking Cross.

"What the fuck are you doing here, Giselle?"

My tone catches the attention of the concierge, who looks between Giselle and me nervously.

"Is everything okay, Mr. Maguire?"

"Everything is fine, Eleanor," Giselle soothes. "We're old friends, isn't that right, Flynn?"

She's looking at me calculatingly, counting on me

not wanting to make a scene, and she knows she has me because the last thing I want is for Wyatt to find out she is here.

"Walk with me." She saunters off toward the lounge area that is set up discreetly in the back corner of the lobby.

I follow uneasily, kneading an anxious palm over my neck, and watch her take a seat as though she doesn't have a care in the world.

"Here." She thrusts the pizza at me. "I had to call in a big avour to make this meeting happen."

"Are you expecting a thank-you because you, what? Bribed some dumb-ass pizza delivery kid? Every delivery kid in the city?" I shake my head. "You're fucking delusional."

"Not a thank-you, no. Just want you to know how dedicated I am, I guess. So." She throws me a sly grin. "A wife, huh?"

"Yep," I bite out, turning away, determined not to give her anything she can use.

"You know, I still remember the first time I saw you on stage. You were hot as fuck, pissed at the world and had sex written all over you. That night was…" She trails off, the silence hanging in the air until I finally look at her. "I guess that makes you a cheater, doesn't it?"

My head snaps back as though I was punched, and I feel like my veins are on fire as I try to control the anger suddenly avouring me.

"We were separated. Now if this trip down memory lane is finished, I have—"

"I helped kickstart your career, you owe me, Flynn. I've given you time, I knew you were going through something. That something significant had happened to you and you were trying to work your way through it. I gave you time to do that." Her eyes narrow with a vicious glint. "And now, after I've waited so patiently for you, you have a fucking *wife*?" Her voice rises, a slight note of hysteria creeping in.

I sit back and look at her dispassionately, remembering that first night we met. Recalling how her formal elegance, her almost icy beauty, was so disparate to the skeevy bar I was playing in. How everything about her seemed to be in such contrast to Wyatt's carefree joy. How I thought maybe, *maybe*, this was exactly what I needed to get over her.

I also remember waking up the next morning, my judgment no longer clouded by cheap whiskey and expansive grief, sneaking out and never giving it a second thought.

"I probably never would have found out about her if you hadn't been so careless when you came to see her, you know." She shakes her head, her voice accusing.

"I wasn't trying to hide her."

"You probably should have." She stands, brushing an imaginary piece of lint from her cashmere sweater. Lifting her eyes, she pins me with a look of contempt. "She's going to hate you by the time I'm done with you."

CHAPTER FIFTEEN

WYATT

"I can't believe I'm in the green room of *The Tonight Show!*" I whisper, practically giddy, but doing my best to hide it. Meanwhile, Flynn sits casually beside me, as though none of this is a big deal. Which, I guess to him, it isn't.

"I love Thomas Carlson so freaking much, I just want to cuddle him."

Flynn's mouth lifts in a small smirk, one of the few smiles I have seen today. He's been in a weird mood since last night and I'm not really sure what is going on.

"Should I be worried you're about to run off with the Englishman?"

I snort out a laugh. "No, I'm much more into bossy, Irishmen, so you have nothing to worry about."

I lean back into the buttery leather cushions of the sofa and watch everything that's going on around me. There are multiple television screens scattered throughout the large room, all secured to walls, so that wherever you are, you can see the show that is currently being filmed. Thomas is interviewing the actor Tucker Royal, and I sigh a dreamy little sigh as I watch the blond Adonis talk about his upcoming movie release.

"The guy's an asshole, you know." Flynn's amused voice draws my attention back to him.

"Meh, but he's a pretty asshole, so he can be forgiven." I laugh with a shrug.

I take hold of Flynn's arm and pull it across my body until my hand finds his and I thread our fingers together.

The room is loud, the guys in his band are congregated around the table, eating their way through the incredible spread that was out. I swear to God, I had the most amazing doughnut I have ever had in my life and I was ready to cut a bitch to find out where I could get my hands on more.

Luckily, it didn't come to that and a very helpful assistant gave me the address, as well as the hot tip that their maple bacon doughnuts are to die for.

Now, this is the type of celebrity perk I could get used to.

I give Flynn's hand a gentle squeeze, relishing the feel of his calloused skin.

"Hey, you okay?" I whisper in his ear, enjoying the slight shiver I note as my breath tickles the spot just below his ear. "You've been quiet."

He pulls our joined hands to his mouth and his deliciously full lips place the softest kiss on my knuckles.

"I'm fine. He's going to ask about us, you know." He

tilts his head toward the screen where Thomas Carlson is delivering a punchline. "He's going to want all the details and I normally give a standard 'no comment.'"

My heart dips a little at that and I have to fight the urge to pout, which is ridiculous, I'm well aware.

"Well, then, that's what you'll do. I can't imagine he'll force the issue unless he wants to make things incredibly awkward."

Flynn watches me closely, his eyes darting over my entire face, a look of curiosity painted across his dark features.

"You want me to talk about us?"

"No," I hastily reply, wondering what he could see in my face. My face that now feels as though it is on fire. "I mean, I guess it would be nice for you to confirm it? I don't want to feel like you're embarrassed to talk about me."

He pulls his hand from mine, and slides it around my shoulders, pulling me to him tighter. "It has nothing to do with being embarrassed, Cherry. But the second I talk about it, that's like announcing open season. They're going to take that as permission to ask about everything, no matter how personal. They're going to use anything I say as an excuse to be as intrusive as possible." He leans down and kisses the tip of my nose. "It's just not worth it."

I listen to what he's saying, and I understand it completely. What he is describing does sound horribly obtrusive. But I also can't deny that the idea of your man declaring his love for you publicly is dangerously intoxicating.

"I get it. That does sound awful, you're right." I force a smile and pray it doesn't look as contrived as it feels.

He studies me again, his eyes questioning, and I know he is about to press the issue. Fortunately, a producer picks this moment to enter and round all the guys up for their performance.

After a quick rundown of the order of what is about to happen, she leads them out to the studio stage. Flynn pauses in the doorway, and looks back at me, his face serious.

"I love you."

This time there is nothing insincere about the smile that lights up my face.

"Love you too. Now, get your ass out there, Irish."

Ten minutes later, I'm close to tears as Flynn plays the final notes of the first single from his upcoming album. It's one of the first songs he wrote after we became an official couple. Slightly tweaked and re-worked, but still the song he wrote all those years ago. Written in his basement while I painted my nails, played around on social media or just sat and watched him. It is a song of idealism and hope; the intensity of first love and the breathtaking *need* for another person.

Hearing him play it after all of these years is eye-opening and I'm overwhelmed with sadness for the teenage us. The "us" that only ever wanted each other and yet, somehow, we lost it all. Those fifteen-year-olds had no idea of the tragedy that awaited them, but right now, I am filled with so much hope that we are going to make it.

That one day the pain of our past will pale in comparison to the light of the life we are going to create together.

I am still feeling emotional when the show returns from the ad break, and Flynn's face fills the screen.

An easy grin breaks across his face as he laughs at something Thomas says and I swallow down the lump in my throat, excited to be a part of this piece of his life for the first time.

The interview is pretty standard, lots of questions about the new music and Flynn tells a story about a practical joke his drummer played during the recording of the album. There's an easy camaraderie between the two men, and when Thomas begins to wrap up the interview, I consider that our earlier conversation was unnecessary. It seems Mr. Carlson rises above inane gossip after all.

I shift in my seat, the leather creaking under me, and wait for the interview to finish.

"So, it would be remiss of me not to mention the extraordinary turn of events in your love life recently."

Well, would you look at that? Not so much rising above after all.

An *"ah fuck"* look flits across Flynn's face and he grimaces.

"Now, c'mon. You know I have to ask. I'd be run out of the late-night talk show hosts union if I didn't," Thomas jokes. "So, spill, how do you suddenly remember you have a wife?"

The audience laughs, and Flynn shakes his head ruefully. I chew nervously on my bottom lip, although why I am nervous, I have no idea, and wait for him to offer up his answering "no comment."

Instead, Flynn pauses, and the entire studio falls silent.

"Nothing sudden about it, Thomas," he replies with an enigmatic smile.

The host seems slightly shocked he didn't just get blown off and he takes a moment to regroup.

"Wait, wait, wait." Thomas waves his hands around. "You realize this is a pretty strange situation, right? You've had a secret wife all of these years, one who no one ever had an inkling about, and then suddenly one day she's all over the internet and you're off the market. How does that work?"

Flynn shifts uncomfortably in his seat, wiping his palms along his jeans. Apart from that small tell, he's looking cool, calm, and collected, but I know how much he hates feeding into this side of the fame machine and I can't figure out why he doesn't put a stop to the discussion.

Until it hits me. Because of me.

My stomach drops as I realize he is doing this for me and I'm somehow simultaneously grateful and horrified.

Flynn's accented rasp grabs my attention and I turn back to the television.

"I understand it's an unusual situation, but I make no apologies for the way I live my life." He shrugs his broad shoulders. "I married the love of my life. I've made plenty of shit decisions since then, obviously, but that has never been one of them."

"Well, that's great to hear, I'm happy for you, I really am." Thomas turns to face the camera, holding up the cover of Flynn's album. "Flynn Maguire's new album, *Reckless Reverie,* is out on Thursday, make sure and grab your copy." He swings back to Flynn and as the studio band starts playing, he leans over and shakes Flynn's hand.

My heart is jackhammering in my chest and despite the mess of emotions ricocheting through me, only one thought is really sticking.

That man is going to get laid tonight.

CHAPTER SIXTEEN

FLYNN

"You ready?" I ask distractedly, pulling my buzzing phone out of my pocket.

"Nearly. Which shoes?" Wyatt comes out of the hotel bedroom, holding up two pairs of black boots.

They both look the same to me, but I am not a stupid man, so I quickly point to the pair on the right. "Those ones."

Wyatt nods nervously, rushing back into the bedroom, leaving me alone for a moment.

Lighting up my screen, I quickly click on the Google alert notification. Tension is thumping along my temples as I wait for the link to Giselle's blog to load. She has posted daily bullshit stories that make me look like a first-class piece of crap, since our altercation over the weekend.

Cam claims to be worried about the effect it might have on album downloads, but we both know that's a load of shit. My name in the headlines, no matter the reason, will only increase the units I sell.

No, the reason she's doing this is to tarnish me in Wyatt's eyes and drive a wedge between us. What she doesn't know is that nobody is more aware of my flaws than Wyatt is, and her dredging up petty-assed stories about women I fucked or asshole comments I made, will not break us.

If she really believes this is all it will take to send Wyatt running, she underestimates both my girl's loyalty and my assholery.

My shoulders relax as I skim today's piece of shit. A re-hashed story from three years ago about a hotel room I allegedly trashed. The real story is that a drummer we brought in for one show when Jett was sick, went on a drug-fuelled bender causing thousands of dollars' worth of damage. Money that I had to pony up for.

But I guess me being the douchebag was a far better story, so that's how it played out in the media.

"Okay, I'm ready. How do I look?" Wyatt stands on her tiptoes, raises her arms, and does a little pirouette.

My eyes rake up the line of her lithe body. She's tall and slender with curves that make my fingers twitch and my cock ache. The short black dress she is wearing shows off her long legs perfectly and I look forward to having them wrapped around my waist later tonight.

Or my head, I'm not fussy.

"Fucking perfect." I pocket my phone and move toward her. "The car will be here in five minutes." I slide the thin strap of her dress aside slightly and place a kiss on her shoulder. "I wonder what we could do for the next five minutes?"

She tilts her head up at me, a sly grin dancing along her full lips, but before she can say anything, there's a loud knock at the door.

"Car's here, Flynn," Zane's voice disrupts us.

My forehead falls gently against hers, a rueful smile in place.

"We could always cancel?"

She laughs, a soft, sultry laugh that makes my stomach clench in anticipation.

"We are not canceling on your friends. We flew out here just to see them," she admonishes.

"No, we're here for interviews. Seeing them was just an afterthought." My mouth trails up the curve of her neck, tasting and kissing. Hopefully, convincing.

"Lies!" She pushes me away, but her hands linger on my chest. "You set up these interviews as an excuse to come back to LA. I'm onto you, Irish." She wags a finger at me. "It's time to feed me and show me off. You can fuck me later." Her fingernails scrape down my chest and she leans up and places a kiss on my throat, right next to my Adam's apple, before she whispers in my ear, "I promise."

Taking a step back, she smiles at me innocently, as though she didn't just get me harder than steel.

"Right, let's get this over with." I grab her hand and drag her toward the door. The sooner we do this, the sooner we'll be back here, and I can be inside her. Which, I'm not going to lie, is my absolute favorite place to be.

"Wait, I need my purse!" She laughs.

I drop her hand and race back to the bedroom and find her purse on the dresser. Snatching it up, I run back to her and resume my race out the door, her hand in mine.

Fifteen minutes later we're in the back seat of the SUV, having survived the media scrum. Zane and Chris are up front, the privacy screen is in place and we're headed out to Pacific Palisades.

"It was quieter than normal."

I look at Wyatt with her flushed cheeks and bright eyes, and I wish that loving me didn't mean having to deal with all of this BS.

"That's good right?" Her voice slightly nervous. "It means they're getting tired of us?"

"Yeah." I take hold of her hand and raise it to my mouth, placing a kiss on her palm. "The story's played out, people don't care anymore. This is more what you can expect on a normal day."

Her brow furrows. "So, wait, they're never all gone?"

I laugh and cringe slightly when I hear the edge of bitterness it holds. "No, there is always someone there, with a camera shoved in your face. You don't always see them, but they're there."

She pulls her hand away, but only so she can trace along my jaw, her fingertips scraping through my stubble. Her eyes are serious, and I wonder if it's finally occurring to her that I might not be worth all the sacrifices it is going to take to be with me.

Instead, she leans in and brushes her lips across

mine.

"I guess we'll have to make sure we give them some-thing worth photographing then."

This fucking woman.

Moving away slightly, she quirks an eyebrow at me.

"Have you seen Giselle's blog this week? There's been something horrible posted about you every day."

I can feel the scowl settle on my face.

"She's a bitch, not even worth worrying about."

"I don't know, it feels like more than that." She shakes her head. "It feels almost personal. How well do you know her?"

I square my shoulders slightly, my body tensing.

"Oh." She purses her lips, nodding. "Right."

"It was a long time ago and a huge fucking mistake." I take her hand and place it between mine, marveling at how well it fits, despite the size difference. But that's us all over. No matter how many differences there are between us, nobody is a better fit for me than her.

"It's fine, Flynn, really. We were separated, we both saw other people and neither of us did anything wrong." She steals my move, taking hold of one of my hands and pulling it to her mouth. Her lips open slightly, and she places a kiss on the back of my hand, right below my thumb. A simple and chaste gesture, but her mouth anywhere on my body sends a frisson of electricity through me.

Pulling away, she moves back, her body turned toward me, her face suddenly anxious.

"So, tell me more about your friends."

She's playing with a strand of her hair, the dark red

a stark contrast to the bright pink of her nails and worrying her bottom lip with her teeth.

"You don't have anything to worry about," I reassure her. "Brax knows all about you. He's been telling me to win you back since I met him, so he's feeling pretty fucking cocky right about now. And Mel loves everyone."

My words were meant to be reassuring, but from the look on her face it had the opposite effect.

"What?"

"He knows all about me?"

"Yeah, we might have gotten a bit drunk the night we met and told each other our biggest secrets. Remind me to tell you about his Disney obsession one day." I snort out a laugh as I remember Brax, six foot two, heavily tattooed and mohawked at the time, confessing his love for Disney movies. *The Little Mermaid* is his favorite, just in case you were wondering.

"But he must hate me!" Wyatt looks horrified and I have no fucking clue why.

"Why would he hate you?" The confusion obvious in my voice.

"Because I was horrible to you. God, I told you it was your fault, Flynn. Who says something like that to someone? Especially to someone they love!"

Her entire demeanor has changed. She's curled into herself and her eyes are full of pain.

"Yeah, you said that." I wrap a hand around her thigh and drag her along the seat until she's right in front of me and then my hands slide up to cup her face. "You were in pain and you needed someone to blame.

That's what lovers do for each other. We take the hit and absorb the pain, so the person we love doesn't have to." I place a kiss on the tip of her nose. "I'll always be sorry that I was too immature to realize that at the time. I did think leaving was the best thing to do for you, but it also gave me an excuse to run from my mistakes. You needed me, and I let you down." I close my eyes and quietly inhale her vanilla scent. "I let you down the night we lost Carys, and I let you down again while you were grieving her. I have no idea why you're giving me another chance, but I'm fucking glad you are."

She tilts her head up until her lips find mine, and she presses a dozen small kisses along them.

"You didn't let me down that night."

"If it wasn't for me you wouldn't have been there. You didn't want to go, I'm the one that forced the issue." My hands grip her hips, trying to center myself as memories of that night rush me. The fear when I saw the flames curling around the stage curtain, already out of control by the time they were noticed. The chaos of the audience all scrambling for the exits and the terrified screams that fixed themselves into my consciousness where they remain to this day.

The immeasurable terror when I couldn't find Wyatt, that never fully subsided because by the time I found her at the hospital, our lives were forever changed.

Wyatt grabs my face and turns it toward her, a determined look on her face.

"You listen to me. I was there that night because I

wanted to be. That's the only reason. We've spent the last ten years rewriting our story and painting ourselves as the villains." She sighs deeply. "Nothing that happened that night was your fault. You're not the bad guy. I was horrible to you, and I hope you really have forgiven me for that, because I am so fucking sorry. But getting lost in my grief and lashing out doesn't make me a bad guy either." She slides across my lap until she is straddling me. "How about we just say that we're human and we fucked up. But there's still plenty of time for us to turn this around and become the heroes we need to be." Her arms wrap around my neck and she pulls me close until we're nose to nose. "I promise to save you if you save me."

I smile against her lips. "Always."

♨

"More popcorn?" Brax yells from the kitchen.

"Braxton Havenworth, inside voice!" Mel whisper-yells back. "You'll wake up Billy."

"Wait, Havenworth?"

Mel turns to Wyatt. "I know, he doesn't look like a trust fund baby, does he? Until you live with him, that is. Then you find out exactly how spoiled his gigantic ass is." She rolls her eyes and I fight back a laugh.

"What's going on?" Brax looks at us all suspiciously when he re-enters the living room.

"You! Serenity by *Havenworth*!" Wyatt points an accusing finger at him. "You were the one responsible for the spa setup!"

"Ah, that." Brax flops down onto the sofa beside his giggling wife. "I was playing cupid and doing it pretty fucking spectacularly. You can thank me anytime."

"He was so damn proud of himself." Mel laughs.

"I don't know why," I huff. "It was all my idea, he was just the connection. Everyone knows I'm the romantic one."

"What!" Brax bolts upright, a look of outraged indignation on his face. "I am absolutely the more romantic one. Babe." He taps Mel's leg in the exact same way Billy does when he's trying to get his mom's attention. "Babe, tell them how I proposed."

"Baby, that story is *not* going to win you any points, try again."

"It was romantic as fuck, what are you talking about?" Brax's eyebrows are furrowed, his mouth turned down and his eyes are screaming confusion. It's almost enough to make you pity the guy.

"Right after we had sex you told me you wanted to make me come every day for the rest of my life, so we should probably get married."

Wyatt and I look at each other, both trying to stifle a laugh. Although, honestly? She is trying a little harder than me.

"*Not* romantic and *not* a story I could tell anyone." Mel pouts before patting his arm. "It's okay, babe, you have other qualities. It doesn't matter if you're not romantic." She offers him a consolatory smile which causes me to lose my last little bit of self-control and a loud laugh rolls through me.

"Shut up, asswipe," he grumbles. "Didn't you

propose at the age of ten or something. I highly doubt your story is more romantic than mine." He turns to Mel with a ridiculous pout. "Which I still say was *totally* romantic bee tee dubs."

Mel and I groan in unison, used to Brax's theatrics, but we are cut off by Wyatt.

"Well, actually," she begins, her face lit up teasingly. "Flynn's proposal was pretty freaking romantic."

"Oh my God, tell us! I bet he was all sullen and moody as a teenager, but with the heart of a poet." Mel kneels up, her body leaning toward Wyatt expectantly while Brax scowls at me across the room.

"You're about to show me up, aren't you?"

"Yup." I smirk at him unapologetically.

"Okay, so there were a few swamps near where we lived and one of them had this rickety-assed wooden pergola alongside it. It was so old and practically falling down, but it was covered in wisteria and every year, without fail, it bloomed these beautiful flowers." She closes her eyes and inhales as though she can smell the scent that used to permeate the air on the nights we lay under it. "It was my favorite spot in the entire world. We would take a blanket and just talk for hours. I fell in love with him under that pergola, breathing in those flowers. It felt..." Her voice trails off and she blushes. "Magical. It sounds corny, but that's the only way I can describe it. Anyway." She shakes her head, a small smile playing on her lips. "One day we were there, it was just an ordinary day. I was sketching, and he was on his guitar, writing lyrics and playing around with a melody." Her eyes meet mine and I know that we're both back in the moment, remembering the moment I made the smartest decision of my life.

"The sun started to set so I began to pack away my stuff when he hands me the piece of paper he had been writing on all afternoon. When I read it, it was a song about us. About us getting married and taking on the world together. It was called 'Partner in Crime' and down the bottom of the page he had written, *I love you. Marry me. Today, tomorrow, or five years from now, I don't care. But say yes.*" She looks at me and smiles so big, she reminds me of that girl beside the swamp, under the wisteria, who hadn't tasted the bitterness of tragedy yet.

"Anyway." She shakes her head with a laugh, turning back to Mel and Brax who are hanging on her every word. "It was the most romantic moment of my life, so I'm pretty sure he has you, Brax. Sorry."

Mel turns to her husband and slaps his arm.

"What was that for?" he shouts.

"For not being more like *him!*" she declares, pointing at me. "No sex for you tonight."

Wyatt giggles as she watches the two of them, but a booming laugh bursts from me when I see the look on his face, like a petulant child who has just been told he can't have any candy.

He looks around the room, slowly taking each of us in, and when his gaze lands on me, his eyes narrow and he glares with the strength of a thousand suns.

"You are dead to me."

CHAPTER SEVENTEEN

WYATT

"This is incredible!" Layla's voice is all squeaky and high, the way it gets when she's excited and her eyes are bouncing all over the place, watching the backstage action that is unfolding around us.

"Bubs." Cassidy nudges her little sister. "Take it down a notch, okay? Let's try and play it a little cool, 'kay?"

"Hell, no. I'm with Lay. This is freaking awesome!"

"Balls!" Cassidy scrunches her nose up as she chastises Skye, who simply shrugs her shoulders and grins.

I look at the three women sitting on a large speaker opposite me, who have become my family since I moved to New York. I cling on to Charlie's hand, who is sitting beside me, grateful that she flew in from Chicago for tonight. I am so fucking lucky to have women like this in my life. Friends who champion me and cherish me, as I do them. I will *never* take that for granted.

"Will we get to see Flynn before the show starts?"

Cassidy laughs at Skye's question causing her to blush a deep rose red, which then has Layla and me in a fit of giggles.

"What am I missing?" Charlie asks.

"Skyeballs has a crush on Flynn. It's equal parts adorable and awkward."

Skye whacks Cassidy on the arm. "I do not!" she argues. "I just really love his music. It makes me think of Ben and..." She trails off, her face lighting up once again, setting us all off this time.

We are getting a lot of curious looks from the roadies rushing past us, so I try to compose myself.

"No, he's with the band right now, but there's going to be a small after-party at *Silhouette* afterward, so you can see him then." I wink at her.

"Oh, I would love to, but I have to get home straight after. Ben's on a business trip so my mom has the girls."

"Ugh, I'm in the same boat." Cassidy groans. "Mason is sick with the manflu and I promised I would get home as soon as possible. Our kids are like lemurs, they can sense weakness."

Layla wiggles in her seat, biting her bottom lip. "I'm out too, I have a ton of paperwork I need to do tonight."

"Nooo, can't you do it tomorrow?" I throw her my best puppy dog eyes.

"I wish I could, but it's Ethan's mom's birthday, so we'll be at their place all day. Adulting blows." She huffs.

"Alright, well then, I guess it's just us." I turn to Charlie. "It'll be just like old times!"

Charlie pulls a face and I immediately know I'm not going to like what comes next.

"I'm sorry, Reeses. I have meetings tomorrow, I need to be on the red-eye tonight."

"But tomorrow is Sunday!"

"I know." She grimaces. "But if I want to make partner, I need to put in the hours." She lays her head on my shoulder. "I'm sorry."

"It's okay." I look around the group. "I might just need to find some new friends though."

"Speaking of new friends, do you remem—"

"Ladies." Charlie is cut off by the arrival of Campbell. "Our suite is ready, shall we?" He motions to a long hallway and we all excitedly jump off the speakers we had parked our asses on.

"So, when does the tour actually start?" Skye asks.

"Why, are you planning on coming back for another go-around?" Cassidy jokes.

"The tour officially kicks off next month in Manchester. But we wanted to do a few early performances here in the States," Cam answers. "He's already done The Hollywood Bowl, tonight's show and then a week before we fly to the UK, he's doing a show at Fenway Park."

Layla sidles up to me, nudging me with her shoulder. "How long is he going to be away for?"

"Oh, uh, the tour goes for three months. He's going around the United Kingdom, Asia, and Australia before he comes home and tours around the US." My hand finds its way into the long strands of my hair, twirling it nervously.

"That's a long time." She frowns. "I don't think I could go that long without seeing Ethan."

"Oh. My. Fleeking. Gooseberry."

A giggle bubbles in my throat, as it always does when I hear Cassidy's kid-friendly cursing, and I can't blame her for her outburst. We have all stopped in the doorway to the luxury suite where we will be watching the concert, our eyes wide in excitement.

There are two rows of golden-brown leather couches facing the floor-to-ceiling window. Two couches on each row, separated by a small aisle, and each one providing ample seating for two people. The leather looks so soft I briefly contemplate rushing over and rubbing my cheek along it. Just for a moment until I come to my senses.

A fully stocked bar stands at the back of the room, just behind a lounge area with more leather sofas and a small coffee table. To the right of the room is a long table holding four covered serving dishes that are providing the most delectable aromas.

Campbell moves confidently into the room, settling himself on a seat and immediately pulling out his cell phone and making a call.

We all look at each other for a split second before we race inside oohing and aahing over everything. When we have cooed over everything in the room, we take a seat at the lounge area, laughing at ourselves.

"We really need to calm down." Skye giggles. "We should be acting like mature adults, not a bunch of tweens who have just spotted BTS."

"Who the fuck are BTS?" Cassidy furrows her brows.

"They're that boyband." Layla groans. "So many of my students are obsessed with them."

"Aren't your students, like, eight?" I ask, pulling down the hem of my blue shirt dress.

"Oh my God, I am dreading reaching that stage with Mack. I already feel like she's three going on sixteen. Mason and I don't stand a chance against her." Cass covers her face with her hands and falls against me. "Hold me, Red. Or better yet, pray for me. I'm going to need it."

"At least I don't need to worry about Summer," Skye pipes up before taking a sip of her soda. "She's already planning her wedding to Seb."

"Could you imagine?" I cry. "How wonderful would that be if they did grow up and get married?"

"Meh, I'm still not sold on being officially related to Spanky."

Skye throws a pretzel across the table at Cassidy. "You should *be* so lucky to be related to my husband, you punk." She laughs.

"Speaking of kids." Charlie turns to Layla. "Wyatt told me about your news, congratulations!"

Layla looks at me apprehensively and I throw her a reassuring smile. "It's fine, Lay. You're allowed to talk about it. I promise, I'm good."

Her shoulders relax instantaneously, and she looks at me gratefully.

"Thank you," she says to Charlie. "We're so excited. I'm a little overwhelmed, especially since my sister insists on telling me what to expect in the birth, in *graphic detail.*" She glares at Cassidy, and Skye, Charlie, and I do the same.

"What? She needs to know! Knowledge is power and all that horsey poo."

"That's just cruel, Cass." Skye takes hold of Layla's hand. "You'll be fine, it's not that bad at all."

Cassidy snorts. Loudly.

Ignoring her, Layla turns to me. "What about you? Have you and Flynn discussed your options for a family?"

After my meltdown when Layla told me about her pregnancy and once I felt like Flynn and I were on solid ground, I confessed my infertility to the girls. It was a difficult discussion, but one I wish we had had years ago. No longer needing to pretend I was okay all the time was life changing.

"We've agreed to look at our options. He wants to start the ball rolling now, but I don't think I'm ready yet." Charlie clutches my hand, offering her support. "It was only a couple of months ago that I had written off the idea of kids. I need a little more time to get my head around the idea that kids might be possible."

My friends are all nodding in understanding and I can feel myself start to get a bit emotional, so I quickly change the subject.

"I can't remember the last time I saw some live music, thank you all for coming with me."

"Please, I'm husband-free, kid-free, and sitting in a luxury suite with a drink in my hand and my best friends by my side. Thank *you.*"

"Truth." Skye raises her drink and cheers Cassidy.

"So, what are you going to do for the three months Flynn's away? You two were never great with the separations."

I raise an eyebrow at Charlie.

"I mean before the last ten years, obviously." She rolls her eyes at me. "Although you both kind of sucked at it then too, if we're being honest."

I stick my tongue out at her, shaking my head.

"I'm actually going to go with him."

My statement is met with silence. I look at each of my friends and their faces are all frozen in some version of surprise.

Cassidy is the first to speak, and she does so with wide eyes. "You lucky bitch."

I laugh as some of my tension eases away.

"I know, I'm so excited, I never dreamed I would get the chance to see the world, especially like *this*."

Layla jumps up from her seat and rushes around to wrap me in a huge bear hug. "I'm so, so happy for you. Nobody deserves this more than you, I hope you know that."

Her whispered words make my eyes sting and I push her away with a big smile. "Don't make me cry," I mumble.

I sit back, sinking lower into the sofa, as my friends begin excitedly talking about the tour, asking questions, and making plans.

For the first time in forever, my heart feels completely free.

"Call me, okay?" Skye's arms squeeze me tight. "We can go out for dinner next week. I want to hear more about the painting you're working on."

"Sounds good." I smile, returning her hug.

"C'mon, Balls, Mason is sending me SOS messages." Cassidy pulls me to her for a quick embrace before climbing into the Uber. "Call me, Red."

"Bye, Wyatt! Talk to you soon," Layla calls from her spot behind Cassidy and Charlie and I wave them all off.

"Miss Reed, the car is ready," Zane interrupts us.

"You really can't stay?" I try to hide my disappointment.

"I'm sorry, I can't." Charlie tucks her long, wavy hair behind her ear and I notice it's darker than the last time I saw her.

I can feel the frown fix on my face. "Am I going to see you before we leave?"

She levels me with a look that tells me everything I need to know.

"You need to stop working so hard, you know that, right?"

"Right." She scoffs. "Nobody makes partner working less than a hundred hours a week, so I don't see that happening anytime soon."

I take her hand, pulling her close to me and then linking our arms as we follow Zane to the waiting car.

"There's more to life than work, Charlotte Reed." I

use my best mother hen voice. "You should try and remember that."

She tilts her head until her temple is resting against mine. "Yes, Mom."

We reach the car and Zane opens the door. I pull Charlie to me in a hug, clutching her to me tightly. "I love you, Pieces."

She holds me with an equal amount of fervor. "Love you too, Reeses."

Pulling back, she shakes her head at me. "I'm so glad you two got your shit together, I mean, you took your sweet-ass time, but better late than never, I guess." She smirks at me as she climbs into the SUV and then blows a kiss before Zane closes the door.

"Miss Monroe?"

I watch the car pull into traffic and a wave of sadness washes over me when I realize I don't know when I'll see her again.

"Please call me Wyatt." I turn to Zane. "What's up?"

"Flynn asked me to make sure you were taken to his dressing room."

"Of course, he did," I reply wryly. "Okay, let's go."

Zane leads us back inside and I follow him through the hallways that lead to the dressing rooms in silence. The man is definitely not a talker.

We're halfway there when Zane's phone goes off. He checks the message and his brows knit together, lips pursed, stopping in the middle of the corridor.

"Are you okay to go the rest of the way by yourself? There's a situation I need to deal with."

"Of course, is everything okay?" I can't help asking because he looks pissed.

"Nothing you need to worry about." He points straight ahead. "Keep going that way and make the next left. Flynn's room is the last one at the end of the hall, he shouldn't be much longer." With that, he turns and strides away in the direction we just came from.

I start walking back toward the dressing rooms, noticing how eerie it feels in here. Where the hell is everyone?

I reach the corner and am just about to turn when a hand wraps around my waist from behind and I scream, as though I have just come face-to-face with the biggest, hairiest spider imaginable.

I start to struggle, but I'm quickly spun around and pressed up against the wall, Flynn's body flush against mine.

He brushes his nose along mine. "Hey, Cherry." His voice is hoarse, as it always is after a show, all gravelly and sexy.

"You scared the shit out of me!" I slap a hand over his bicep. He's shirtless, the grey t-shirt he wore during the performance slung around his neck, a sheen of sweat sticks to his skin.

My hands itch to touch him, so I do just that, because why would I resist? I glide my hands down his chest, lightly scratching across his nipples and contin-uing down to tease my fingertips through his happy trail.

His eyes fall closed and he groans, pressing his hips

forward so his cock creates the perfect amount of friction in the most perfect spot.

Flynn's mouth glides along my jaw, his tongue teasing, and I press my thighs together, my panties becoming uncomfortably damp.

"You want me to fuck you right here, baby?" He palms my breasts and pinches my nipples sending the most glorious sensations rioting through my body. "Fuck you where anyone could find us?"

I'm incapable of speaking at this point, so I answer in the only way I can. I drop my hands to the button on his jeans and quickly free him, wrapping my hand around his shaft and jerking him off.

He thrusts into my hand and his mouth takes mine in a ferocious kiss. A kiss that leaves me breathless and wanting. My tongue tastes him, demanding more, while I savor the feel of his fingers that have found their way into my panties, circling my clit.

The need for him to be inside me is devastating.

"Flynn," I murmur against his mouth. "Fuck me, now."

He pulls away from me, a smirk on his face. "You gonna say please?"

My eyes narrow in a glare at the smug bastard. He thinks he has the upper hand? We'll see.

I lift my leg and wrap it around his waist, bringing his cock to my core and sliding his thick head along my slit. I place the tip at my opening and can't hide the smile when his head falls to my shoulder with a loud groan.

His hand grips my thigh, holding it in place, and

with no further warning, he thrusts forward, seating himself fully and pinning me to the wall with his hips.

"Fuck, your pussy feels so good." He pulls out before slamming back in.

It's fast and almost brutal, our need for each other only heightened by the risk of getting caught.

With his mouth on my throat and a thumb pressing on my clit, I feel myself tighten around him and I have to bite down on his shoulder to keep from screaming out.

He follows soon after, pressing himself into me deeply and filling me with a loud grunt.

After a moment of time where our harsh breaths and hammering hearts are all that can be heard, Flynn lifts his head with a grin.

"Well, that was fun."

❦

An hour later I step out of his dressing room, ready to head to the Green Room and meet the others before we leave for the after-party. After two more orgasms, I had to begrudgingly leave Flynn in the shower or we would never get out of here.

Throwing my phone in my purse, I turn and almost run right into someone. I start to apologize when I realize who it is and instead a scowl settles on my face.

"What the hell are you doing here, Giselle?"

"I just wanted to stop by and congratulate Flynn on a great show." She pauses, and I notice a hardness to her eyes that wasn't there the last time I saw her. "But I guess you already took care of that."

"Yes. I did. Because I'm his *wife*."

I start to push past her, but she grabs my arms, stopping me.

"I was so sorry to hear about your daughter. Carys, was it?"

I feel as though I have been punched in the gut, and I stumble backward slightly.

"What do you want, Giselle." My voice is shaky. "What do you *really* want?"

"I want Flynn." She says it calmly as though it's the most obvious thing in the world, and for the second time in thirty seconds, my gut is churning.

"You want Flynn?" My words come slowly, my brain still trying to make sense of this. "We're married, Giselle, so I guess this is where you learn that you don't always get what you want."

"Oh, but I do. I always get what I want." Her face is expressionless and it's almost frightening.

"I have a deal for you, Wyatt." She takes a step toward me and I instinctively step back. "You leave Flynn, and I make sure no one ever finds out about your tragedy. You stay with him and your worst nightmare is splashed all over the internet, the magazines. It plays out on all the entertainment news channels and that's exactly what your baby's death becomes. Entertainment." She shakes her head. "Is he really worth it?"

Before I can reply she urges me to, "think about it." Then she turns and walks away, leaving me standing there with my life crumbling down around me.

CHAPTER EIGHTEEN

FLYNN

My arm is numb. Pinned under Wyatt and holding her to me, it's doing its job, but I haven't been able to feel it for the last ten minutes. Giving up on the idea of not waking her, I make a fist a few times, trying to bring the feeling back.

My movement jostles her and she moves slightly, pushing back against me so my morning wood is nestled in between her ass cheeks, giving him all kinds of interesting notions. Maybe if I just moved this way—

"Don't even think about it, Irish."

Her morning voice is all throaty and sexy as fuck, and my dick isn't the only one with some interesting ideas, but before I can start anything, Wyatt turns to face me, her expression grim.

"Do you think she'll post it today?"

To say I was furious when Wyatt told me about her altercation with Giselle last night, would be the biggest understatement that had ever been understated in the history of understatements.

I was livid and ready for blood.

Thank fuck one of us has an ounce of sense, because Wyatt was able to talk me off the ledge and realize that Giselle had fucked up by warning her. The point of this whole thing is to hurt Wyatt, to drive her away, but now that she knows it's coming, my girl has her armor up and is ready to fight.

We called Campbell right away and explained the situation to him. I think he might have been as angry as I was if that was possible. Although, to be fair a lot of his pissiness was directed at us, frustrated that we had left ourselves open to this situation when he could have protected us. But he immediately launched into action, setting up an interview with Ophelia Winters, so we can get ahead of the story.

"I think her plan would have been to wait a few days, maybe a week, to see if you followed through." I run my thumb along her cheek, enjoying the softness of her skin. "But she has sources everywhere in this industry and knows everything that goes on. My guess is that as soon as Cam started calling people last night to organize the interview, she would have found out." I cup her face in my hands and place a soft kiss on the corner of her mouth. "I would bet my life that our misery is entertaining the masses right fucking now."

She presses her body into me, her head nuzzling in under my chin.

"I feel like I'm completely prepared and completely

unprepared to deal with this all at the same time." She groans against my skin.

"We got this, Cherry. We'll do the interview, give people our side and make it fucking clear what we think of scum like Giselle who feeds off other people's grief, and then we shut the fuck up." I kiss the top of her head. "It'll be news for a few days until the next DUI or affair hits the headlines, and then no one will give a fuck anymore."

"You're probably right."

"No, I am right. I'm always right, babe. You should know that by now."

She rolls her eyes at me. So fucking cute.

"I think I'll call the girls and see if they—"

The sound of banging on the door interrupts her and she looks at me with wide eyes.

"It'll be Cam." I sit up and look for my jeans from last night, which I hurriedly pull on. My stomach is churning, and I have a horrible feeling that the shit is about to hit the fan. "Take your time getting ready." I lean over and place a chaste kiss on her cheek, only to have her take hold of my face and bring my mouth to her own. Her lips graze mine, her tongue sliding along the seam before she slips it into my mouth, kissing me deeply. A breathy whimper escapes her, and I pull away, knowing that if I don't put a stop to this now, thirty seconds from now, I won't be able to.

"Get ready." I slap her ass, hard, with a smirk and make my way to the door, where, I'm assuming, Cam is still hammering away.

"Relax." I swing the door open. "Jesus, Cam, Give us a minute, it's only seven in the fucking morning."

"Have you seen it?" He pushes past me, cell phone in hand, and my stomach drops.

"How bad is it?"

He hands me his phone, Giselle's blog already pulled up and a scowl settles on my face as I quickly scan the story.

"This is fucking bullshit," I bark. "There's not one shred of truth in there."

I toss his phone on the sofa and begin pacing the room. Blood is pulsing through my veins, and the rush of it is all I can hear.

Abortion.

They're saying Wyatt terminated our pregnancy out of spite because I had an affair.

Giselle has painted her as some kind of psychotic bitch who got rid of our baby for revenge; and I am a cheating douchebag who did the dirty on his pregnant wife.

She's taken us both down with one story.

Motherfucker.

"It's everywhere," Campbell tells me, mirroring my pacing on the other side of the room. "It's been picked up by every entertainment news site."

"It's bad, isn't it?"

We both turn to see Wyatt standing on the threshold of the living room, her eyes dim, and her arms wrapped around her torso, hugging herself.

"She's saying you had a termination." Campbell's voice is impassive. Straightforward and to the point has always been his modus operandi, and I don't think I have ever resented it as much as I do right now when I see the look of unadulterated devastation on my girl's face.

"Jesus, Cam." I move across the room, reaching her in six short strides that seem to take six long hours, and pull her to me, holding her tight.

I feel her chest rising and falling as she tries to catch her breath. She curls into me, grasping my arms, but despite this appearance of vulnerability, when she looks over my shoulder and speaks to Campbell, her voice is strong. The take-no-prisoners Wyatt I fell in love with all those years ago.

"I would never do that. *Never.* You get your ass out there and you make sure there is no one on this *planet* who doubts that. Do you understand me?"

My ears are filled with the sounds of a soaring orchestral score that I'm considering incorporating in the song I am currently writing, but my eyes are glued to Wyatt.

Her easel is set up in front of the window overlooking Central Park and her hand is moving at a lightning pace, the brush making dramatic strokes across the canvas. Despite the brightness of the scene before her, her depiction is dark and powerful.

Her back is straight, shoulders tense, and she has her earphones in, using music to silence the world around her.

The last two weeks have been a fucking nightmare. Our interview made no impact at all. Apparently, the idea of us as two lust-fuelled psychotics, who were driven to extremes in order to torment each other, was a much more believable story than two kids who experienced a life-changing loss.

Wyatt has been doing her best, but I see how much she's struggling. Every whispered comment has her eyes dimming a little more. Every blazing headline sends her retreating into her art.

I'm terrified I'm going to lose her again and that fear means that I have spent the last two weeks angry as hell, ready to lash out at whoever pisses me off.

The only thing that centers me is getting my hands on Wyatt.

I remove my headphones and stalk toward her. When I wrap my hands around her waist and place a kiss on her neck, she startles.

Quickly recovering, she hits my arm with her paintbrush, leaving a streak of deep violet behind, and laughs.

"You scared me, you dick."

I chuckle against her shoulder, breathing in her perfumed skin, that evokes the memory of roses, wisteria, and spice. It's uniquely her and it soothes my chaotic heart.

"That looks incredible." I nod toward her painting, pulling her back against me.

"Mmmm," she murmurs before she starts chewing on the end of the paintbrush, thoughtfully.

"You doing okay?" My lips graze her lobe and I bite down gently.

She shivers, then sighs softly, leaning back into my hold. "You don't have to keep asking me that, you know."

"Yeah, I know. This just— It sucks, and I feel responsible for it all, so I want to make sure you're doing okay." I slide her hair across her shoulder, exposing her neck and admiring the contrast between the vivid hue of her hair and her pale skin. "I'm always going to make sure you're okay, you're gonna have to get used to it."

She balances the paintbrush along the top of the easel and turns to face me, her arms winding around my neck. Standing on her tiptoes, she leans up and kisses my chin.

"This has been so much harder than I thought it would be, I'm not going to lie. There are times when the things they're saying just— It hurts, Irish. In a place I didn't think I could be hurt anymore. But..." Her hands slide up to hold my face in place, so I'm looking her right in the eye. "This is *not* your fault. The only person responsible for this shit show is that bitch and karma will take care of her, I have no doubt."

When her mouth takes mine, I sink into the kiss and try to ignore the sliver of doubt I saw in her eyes.

"You sure you're good?"

Her eyes snap to me in frustration. "Yes, I'm good, will you stop asking me that!"

My shoulders ache, they're so tight with tension. I should be enjoying the sight of my girl. Dripping in diamonds and in a dress that shows off every damn one of her curves, she's almost as beautiful as when she first wakes up in the morning. But I've been fucking dreading this night since we made the decision to come three days ago and I'm still not convinced it was the right choice.

Movie premieres are the stuff of my nightmares to begin with. Add in that we're still in the midst of a publicity storm and it all just creates one solid night clusterfuck.

The red carpet was probing question after none-of-your-fucking-business question. Then we had to watch some shitacular movie and now we're in the middle of a *Temerity Press* party where we're being watched by about twenty bottom-feeding photographers and being whispered about by Hollywood's elite.

A fun night all around, you might say.

But Campbell insists that this is what we need. To see and be seen as they say, so we're trusting his judgment and hoping this isn't the first time he fucks everything up.

I follow Wyatt as she leads us into the center of the room. Our hands entwined, she weaves us through the clustered groups, ignoring the sidelong glances and hushed whispers that are somehow all I can see and hear.

We're almost across the room when we hear it. A

voice rings out above the others and I watch as Wyatt flinches, her shoulders hunching and an air of defeat blanketing her.

"She's going to burn in hell for what she did."

She turns to face me, and I swear to God, it's as though she is moving in slow motion. I know what's about to happen before her eyes even meet mine and I have no fucking way to stop it.

"I can't do this, I'm so sorry." The tears that cling to her lashes are my undoing and I hate myself so fucking much for putting her in this situation. "I tried, Flynn, I really tried, but it's too much."

I see the cameras start flashing in my peripheral vision and all I can focus on is how much she's going to hate seeing this image everywhere tomorrow. Her broken, breaking me.

The whispered murmurs grow louder as the crowd realizes what is going on. The train wreck they're getting to witness firsthand.

I grab Wyatt's arm, determined to end this. To tell her she doesn't need to do this, but she wrenches free.

"You were right. With you, I'll never be free of the past. There will always be a reminder. Some article or rumor." Tears are sliding freely down her cheeks now and I have to use all of my restraint not to reach out and touch her. "I can't do it." She pauses before shaking her head emphatically.

"I *won't* do it."

CHAPTER NINETEEN

WYATT

I close my eyes and try to sleep, but all I see is his face. The pain that emanated off him as my words crushed him.

I know I have done the right thing, the only thing I could do, but it doesn't make it any less painful.

Today has been the most difficult day yet. I woke up this morning in Skye's spare bedroom, to find my face plastered all over the internet again. It's just as jarring as it was the first time. I immediately turned my phone off and hid away, taking refuge in the company of Summer and Poppy and insisting Skye and Ben take advantage of my presence to have a day date.

It took some convincing, but once they were sure I wasn't about to collapse in a heap of emotional despair, they took off for a movie. Babysitting offered a great distraction, and I found myself watching the girls curiously, listening to Poppy's evolving language and marveling at Summer's confidence. As always, I found myself considering what Carys would have been like at that age. If she would have looked like Flynn or taken after me.

I don't think I will ever stop wondering.

But now, in the quiet of the night, I can't stop my brain from going into overdrive as I turn over yesterday's events.

As hard as this is, I have to have faith in my judgment and trust that I am doing the right thing.

It's the only choice I have.

❧

"Get your butt over here, Reeses."

I drop my carry-on at my feet and let Charlie wrap me up in a hug.

"I'm glad you're here."

I sigh and sink into her arms. "I wish it was under better circumstances."

"Meh, I'll take you whichever way I can get you. Is this all you brought?" She picks up my bag and I nod. "Alright, let's get out of here."

I pull my cap down low over my head, feeling completely ridiculous but not enough to risk getting recognized.

We walk to the parking lot in silence. I'm lost in my thoughts and, if I know Charlie, her mind is already off planning her next fancy lawyer move so she can dominate law the way she dominates everything in her life.

"I'm just up here." She points up ahead and to the

left and I do a straight-up double take, laughing for the first time in too long.

"A Prius? Girls from Texas don't drive Prius."

She glares at me and pokes her tongue out. "Shut it." She huffs before mumbling something under her breath.

"What was that?" I giggle.

"I *said*, it gets excellent gas mileage, okay? Now get in the damn car."

The drive to Charlie's apartment is a quiet one. Old school Backstreet Boys plays softly in the background and I lose myself in the scenery as the streets of Chicago rush by.

"How long do you think you'll be staying?" Her voice startles me.

I sigh softly. "I'm not sure. This wasn't in the plan."

"There was a plan?" She snorts, and I smile wryly.

"I'm kind of making it up as I go now."

"Are you sure you're doing the right thing?"

"I didn't have a choice, Charlie." My voice is slightly too insistent, because only forty-eight hours later, I'm not entirely sure that's true.

"Did he get the papers?"

"He did."

"How is he?"

"Don't worry about him, let me worry about him." Campbell's voice is stern, and I've had just about enough with his attitude.

"This is hard for me, Cam. I know your first priority is Flynn, but this is hurting me too."

"You made your decision and now you need to stick to it. Going back and changing your mind is only going to hurt him more, you need to remember that." There's a pause and I hear Simon's voice in the background. Cam sighs and his voice softens. "I know this is hard, Wyatt, but it will get easier and one day you'll be looking back and wondering why you ever doubted yourself."

"I love him." My voice cracks and my throat tightens as I force the words out, knowing that's not what he wants to hear.

"If you love him, you need to be strong enough to do what's right for him."

The bed creaks under me as I roll over, desperate for some sleep.

It's been four days since I forced the world's eyes on us.

Four days of lies.

Four days of hiding.

Four days of regret.

My mind never stops racing and I haven't been able to sleep properly since this all happened. Since before that, if I'm completely honest.

My phone starts vibrating on the side table, and when I reach over and look at the screen, the picture

Flynn took of us that first night we reconnected is lighting up the screen.

I reject the call, knowing that I can't risk talking to him and try to ignore the pain that ricochets through me, but it's useless.

I'm simply going to learn how to live with it until the moment comes that I can breathe again.

CHAPTER TWENTY

FLYNN

Seventeen days.

Seventeen fucking days since I've seen her. Smelled her. Tasted her.

Divorce papers landed on my doorstep thirteen days ago and it's been a complete and total shit show ever since.

Paparazzi out the front of our building scavenging for the best photo, story after story about what supposedly happened between us and I'm so ready to be fucking done with it all.

The amber liquid in my glass swishes as I bring it to my mouth and swallow it down in a single gulp, slamming it back down on the bar.

"Another," I demand.

The bartender looks at me questioningly, but he must see something that warns him off because he moves away and starts pouring my drink.

I look over my shoulder and take in the dive bar I found my way to tonight. A row of sad, drunk bastards line the bar, and to my left, there is a group of wannabe bikers playing pool. I snort into the fresh drink that has been handed to me as I watch them. A bunch of pussies who would probably piss in their pants if someone started something with them.

Some poor asshole is on stage singing and being ignored.

I remember playing that same stage, being over-looked in exactly the same way.

Ah, good times.

"I remember the first time I saw you up there."

Her voice sets my nerves on edge and I have to suck down my drink just to keep from saying something I would regret.

Moving on my barstool, I pull my phone out of my back pocket and place it on top of the bar before I turn to face her.

"What the fuck do you want?"

"Aw, why so blue, sugarpie?" She smirks at me. "No, actually, scratch that. I know exactly why you're so glum." A laugh falls from her lips. "Such a shame that horrible story broke, but I have to admit, I thought she would stick it out longer. I didn't expect her to give up on you so soon. I guess whoever spread the story did you a favor." She shrugs. "She was never going to be around for the long haul."

"And you would be, I suppose." My tone is derisive, and I make no effort to hide it.

"Oh, honey, I don't want you anymore." She lifts the wine glass she has been cradling to her mouth, taking a tiny sip. "I came to my senses and moved on."

"She told me what you did, you know."

The glass stills midway to her mouth before she shrugs and places it back on the bar. When she looks at me this time, all humor is gone.

"When you guys started planning the interview straight after our little chat, I figured she had opened her big mouth." She waves a hand around, waving me off. "It's not a big deal, Flynn. I wanted something, and I went after it. She called me on it and I followed through. It's not my fault if she can't handle the heat. It wouldn't have been the last time her name was dragged through the mud if she stayed with you."

Every one of my pulse points are pounding painfully and I have to grip the bar to keep me on my barstool.

"Only because assholes like you don't consider the truth an important part of any story. But, no." I shake my head. "That's not what I'm talking about."

I see her in the corner of my eye. Her hands that had been playing with her glass, freeze, and her entire body becomes rigid.

"She told me how you threatened to accuse me of raping you if she didn't leave me. How you told her you would destroy my career, *my fucking life*, if she didn't do it." I stop, unable to continue. My hands are shaking as the rage I felt that night returns. "What kind of bitch are you?"

My question is met with silence. A single beat that allows doubt to worm its way into my consciousness.

I shouldn't have worried.

"Me?" she hisses. "What about *you*? I waited for you

all of those years and you led me on, you son of a bitch. All of those exclusive stories. The smiles. All those times you just *happened* to brush up against me." The soft lighting above the bar gives her an almost ethereal quality that is such a contradiction to the venom illuminating her eyes. "You made me believe you wanted me and then you just tossed me aside when *she* came along."

She's a fucking psycho, that's the only explanation for the line of bullshit she's spinning.

"We fucked. Once. I never gave you a second thought after that." I lean toward her and level her with a scowl. "These delusions you chose to believe have nothing to do with me. You're fucking crazy."

"*I am not crazy!*" She slams a hand on the bar and I watch uneasily as my phone jumps on the hard surface.

"Did you tell her you would accuse me of rape, or not? I want the truth, Giselle. You got what you wanted, you've ruined my life. The least you can do is tell me the truth."

"Oh my God, yes, okay? Yes, I told her I would tell everyone you raped me, does that make you feel better?" she sneers. "I watched poor little Wyatt's heart break right in front of my eyes and it was delicious. The way her chin quivered when I told her she couldn't have you either." Giselle's eyes glaze over, and a small smile plays across her lips. "She told me no one would believe me, but I assured her they would. That my reputation in this industry is stellar, and if I said that you had held me down and forced yourself on me, your hand on my neck choking me, then people would believe it. And if not..." She shrugs. "There was always the photos I had doctored up of my 'injuries.'" She giggles as she makes air quotes, but as quick as the laugh appeared, it's replaced with a vicious glare. "God, I can't believe she told you the truth and then she *still* left you. What a bitch."

"She didn't leave me."

"Look who's delusional now." She scoffs. "She dumped your ass in front of a pack of photographers. You know"—she waves a teasing finger in front of me —"you should really thank me for showing you her true colors."

"She didn't leave me. We just wanted you to think she did. So we could get this." I reach across the bar and pick up my phone, turning off the recording and quickly emailing the file to Campbell. "You made it difficult, I'll give you that. Wyatt was supposed to do this, but when you wouldn't take her calls we had to change our plans, file fucking divorce papers to draw your evil ass out." I grimace. "I've been trying to stumble across you for two weeks now. I was actually beginning to think we had gone through all of this bullshit for nothing, but I should have had more faith in your assholishness." I shake my head with a sneer. "You were always going to track me down so you could gloat. What would have been the good in your fucked-up plan if you didn't get to see me suffer firsthand?"

Giselle is staring at me, her face frozen in a mask of horror and I force myself to take a moment to enjoy her comeuppance.

"What are you going to do with that?"

"What am I going to do with it? Campbell is probably emailing it to every entertainment news network as we speak. We are going to make sure everyone hears it, so they all know what a deranged bitch you are." I stand, eager to get out of here and far away from her. "Your career is over, Giselle. Wyatt and I win."

Then I turn and walk away, ready to go and get my girl.

CHAPTER TWENTY-ONE

WYATT

Three weeks ago...

I lean back on my stool and a small sigh slips past my lips as I stare at the canvas in front of me. It's beautiful, I'm objective enough to see that. The darkness of the last few weeks is lifting, and some lightness has made its way onto the canvas. My art has always been a reflection of my heart and I'm relieved to see, as well as feel, that I am coming out on the other side.

All of this Giselle bullshit has only made Flynn and me stronger, our commitment more fierce. We are going to make this work, I've never been more certain of anything. It's as though the hand that has been squeezing the life out of my heart for all of these years has finally lost its grip and I can finally breathe easily again.

I move to pick up the canvas when I'm startled by a low whistle of appreciation from behind me.

"*You are talented, I'll give you that.*"

I turn and my stomach drops when I see Giselle standing in the doorway. Squaring my shoulders, I stand and turn to face her. My hands land on my hips and I can feel my eyes narrow,

"*How did you get in here?*" *I know for a fact Zane is out front and Connor is standing guard out back. There is no way in hell either of them would let Giselle anywhere near me.*

"*Sweetheart, I can get in anywhere I want. Everyone has a price, and I am more than willing to pay. The owner of this building was surprisingly amenable to my offer.*" *She smiles, but it fails to reach her eyes and the result is one of menace.* "*I wonder if you'll be as open to my proposition.*"

Clenching my teeth, I step away from my easel, trying to figure out how quickly I can get all of my stuff out of this art studio. The dream art space that Flynn rented for me only weeks ago, the one that earned him the blow job of the decade, has suddenly lost its sparkle.

I move toward the cubby at the rear of the studio that holds my purse. "*I'm not leaving him. I thought that would have been clear after your last pathetic attempt at blackmailing me.*"

"*Oh, but I think you will,* Cherry." *She spits the name out with venom.* "*And let me tell you why.*"

Ten minutes later, I am standing shell-shocked, watching Giselle's retreating form, wondering how anyone could possibly be so evil.

But if she thinks I'm going to roll over and let her malicious ass get what she wants, she doesn't know me very well.

She'll figure it out soon enough, though.

❧

I pace the room anxiously, waiting for Flynn to get here. My fingers twisted in the oversize t-shirt I was sleeping in when I got the call, I'm waiting for this whole nightmare to finally be over. Campbell's last message said he would be landing forty-five minutes ago and there's a high chance that there will be a hole in Charlie's rug by the time he gets here.

Tired of staring at the walls in the living room, I head into the kitchen to make a coffee. Not because I want one, but because I need to have something to concentrate on other than the clock.

I have just taken the milk out of the refrigerator when the pounding on the front door starts and I drop the carton, watching the creamy liquid spread across the floor.

Choosing to believe that Charlie will forgive me for the mess, I turn and sprint to the door, yanking it open.

Before I can speak, I'm pushed backward and pressed against the wall. Flynn's mouth crashes to mine, his tongue teasing, as he kisses me fiercely. His hands cup my face, holding me in place, and when we finally break apart, he sweeps his thumbs over my skin, gently tracing the slope of my cheekbones.

"Did you get it? Is it over? Did you really get it? She confessed?" My words are expelled in a rush.

"I got it." The heat of his lips kisses a line along my

jaw. "She confessed, it's over," he whispers against my skin before he suddenly pulls away.

"Why the hell weren't you taking my calls?" He grips my thighs and lifts me until my legs wrap around his waist and we're nose to nose.

"Because you would have tried to talk me into coming home, and I would have let you." I pepper his face with kisses. "Cam was right, we needed to be away from each other for it to work."

"I disagree, and now, I think you must be punished." He bites down on the juncture where my neck and shoulder meet, and I can't control the groan that escapes.

"Promises, promises."

I really should know better than to antagonize the beast, because the next minute I'm lifted up, my legs wrapping instinctively around his waist, and the sting of his hand on my ass is all I can feel.

On second thought, antagonizing the beast is kind of fun.

I lift my chin slightly and our mouths are only an inch apart. I can feel his warm breath dance across my lips, and I don't think I have ever been more desperate for the taste of him.

He dips his head, breaching the space between us and I have what I want. His tongue sliding against mine, his mouth devouring me.

He begins to walk, and I feel like I'm floating, too wrapped up in the sensations of him and me together, to worry about something as mundane as how I'm getting from one spot to the other.

I expel a tiny moan when he breaks our connection, and my hands slide into his hair, ready to pull him back to me and finish what we started.

"Where's your fucking room?" His voice is pained, and it forces my eyes open, to see that instead of taking the turn at the end of the hallway that would take us to my bedroom, he has brought us to the kitchen.

"Other way." I tap his chest and nod toward the way we just came.

"When will Charlie be home?"

"She's not coming back, she's in Seattle on business."

My breaths are coming fast and hard and I note with delight the way his eyes fall to my chest.

"Then this will do."

Before I can question what he means, we're moving again and my ass is unceremoniously dumped on Charlie's tiny kitchen table, causing it to wobble slightly. We both pause waiting to see what will happen, but the table steadies underneath me, and I breathe a sigh of relief.

"If we break her table, we'll have to replace it," I warn.

His hands are sliding up my thighs, dragging my t-shirt up until his thumbs are tracing along my panties. So close to where I need them. But not nearly close enough.

"I'm rich, I'll buy her twenty fucking tables and it'll be totally worth it."

He says this with a smirk that is just begging to be kissed. So, I do.

Deep and hard and perfect.

His tongue is meeting mine, stroke for stroke. One hand has my panties pulled to the side, a finger circling my clit in a way that has my knees tightening against his hips, while the other has my ass in a grip that I'm sure will leave fingerprints tomorrow.

My hands wander to his jeans, almost lazily until he pushes his cock against me, and I feel how hard he is.

Suddenly, my movements are almost frenzied as I desperately open his jeans and free him, his cock pulsing in my hand, the tip an angry red. I move my hand, jerking him off a couple of times, loving the feel of him.

How long has it been since I've had my hands on him?

It will never be this long again.

He groans into my mouth and I slip my hand around to his ass, pulling him to me. There's a bereft moment when his fingers leave me and I scoot myself forward, almost unconsciously seeking his touch, only to be rewarded by the broad tip of him as he slowly enters me.

I'm so wet, and the room is so quiet, that all I can hear is the sound of him thrusting into me. The force of each movement rattling the table and eliciting a grunt from him and a small moan from me.

His head is tucked into my neck, and he still has one hand on my ass, dragging me to meet him every time he slams forward. The other hand snakes up under my tee and finds my breast, tweaking my nipple in a way that creates a deep thrum in my clit.

It's the perfect storm of sensation and I'm so close to coming, hovering right on the precipice, when he drives himself into me, burying himself so deep that it tips me over the edge, and I come with a resounding scream.

He lets loose with an almost feral grunt. One that has my fingers digging into his hips, trying to bring him even closer. I feel him filling me up as he comes, his breath harsh and ragged in my ear.

As I cling onto him, waiting for my breath to slow and steady, a small smile plays across my lips and I mark this down as a promise kept.

❧

Three months later...

The small pergola is exactly the same as it was all those years ago. The bloom of the wisteria beautifully woven around the wooden beams, creating an intoxicating perfume that lingers in the air.

I stand on the periphery of the group, thankful that my arrival has gone unnoticed. Grateful I have this moment to quietly observe the people I love as they wait to witness a moment I was too scared to dream of for so long.

Suddenly, a booming voice calls out over the quiet murmurings, drawing everyone's attention.

"You think I don't know you're back there? Get your ass down here, Cherry."

Heads swivel in my direction and I note the smiling faces as my gaze sweeps across the crowd to the man who is waiting for me to recommit my life to him.

"Calm yourself, Irish." I laugh. "We've got forever."

EPILOGUE

FLYNN

*T*en *Years Later*

The room is quiet, depressingly quiet, and completely in opposition to what I know must be going on through the swinging doors to our right, and down that long, seemingly never-ending, corridor.

I shift uncomfortably on the hard, plastic chair, my knee bouncing nervously.

"Stop."

Wyatt's warm hand lands on my knee, squeezing gently and forcing my leg to still.

"It's okay, Irish. We're nearly there, it's nearly over." Her small smile is nervous, and I know she's as anxious as I am. Reaching over, I take hold of her face and bring it to meet mine in a kiss that settles us both. Leaning her head against my own, she sighs deeply.

The elevator to our left pings open and an older couple exits, walking excitedly past us, a giant bouquet dominated by purple shades of wisteria in the man's hands. They head down the hallway, guided by the signs on the wall, as memories of my wife sobbing alone, mourning the loss of our daughter crowd out the excitement from my mind, filling it with anxiety.

I don't get nervous often. I can only think of two occasions. The first, twenty years ago when we stood in a tiny chapel getting ready to commit to each other for the rest of our lives. I was sure she would come to her senses and make a run for it and I was ready to chase.

The second was ten years ago when I thought I was going to lose her again.

Right here, right now I am just as fearful. This moment has been years in the making. We've struggled through the lowest of the lows to get here but we made it, together, and today we finally get to experience the highest of the highs.

If only we can make it through the next few hours.

Wyatt's phone goes off for the millionth time drawing a groan of frustration.

"I wish we had something to tell them."

"Shut it off. They can suffer update-free just like w—"

I'm cut off by the sound of the doors swinging open and a nurse strides out, heading straight for us. Wyatt jumps up, but I can't seem to make my legs work, so I remain sitting, my chest tightening while I wait for the news.

"Mr. and Mrs. Maguire?"

"Yes, that's us. Is it over?" Wyatt trips over her words, anxious to be soothed by this stranger.

"It is. Congratulations, guys, it's a girl. You have a daughter."

A breath I didn't realize I was holding escapes me and I slump forward, elbows on knees, face in hands.

Wyatt rushes the woman, squealing excitedly and wraps her up in a hug much to the amusement of the seasoned nurse.

Abruptly pulling back, Wyatt sobers. "And, Sammi? She's okay? She hasn't—" She chokes up, because we've been here before. So close to completing our family, only to have it ripped right out from under us.

The woman, whose name tag reads Heather, smiles warmly at us.

"Sammi is fine, she's been taken to recovery and she'll be ready to go home in a day or two. She's already said her goodbye to the baby and asked me to tell you one thing."

I find my feet and surge up, wrapping Wyatt in my arms protectively and I feel her tense under me.

"What did she want to tell us?" Her voice is barely a whisper.

"She wanted you to know that she's so happy she chose you."

Rivulets of tears slide along Wyatt's cheeks and I pull her in to me, her face nuzzling my neck as years of fear and frustration finally seep out.

"When can we see her?" I rasp out.

"It shouldn't be too long, how about you go and tell

all your friends and family the good news and by the time you're done, your daughter should be waiting for you."

Five minutes later we are walking into the small waiting room that is filled to the brim with everyone we love. A low-level hum buzzes through the room, hushed voices chatting while children play quietly or sleep in their parent's arms. The sight fills me with peace and we stand for a moment, just taking it all in.

Until an almighty shriek startles everyone and Cassidy rushes over.

"Girl or boy?"

"It's a girl." Wyatt grins.

My mom and Wyatt's parents race over, wrapping us up in hugs, whispering words of congratulations and excitement and I realize that we weren't the only ones living through this nightmare.

I look around the room, seeing our parents, Brax, Mel, Campbell, Simon, Skye, Ben, Cassidy, Mason, Layla, Ethan, Charlie, and Miles, and I feel their enthusiasm, their love, and I realize how lucky we are to have all of them in our lives.

Dragging my wife away from the scrum of people, we send them on their way with promises to send photos as soon as we can and let them know when we're ready for visitors.

"She's so beautiful."

We're curled up on the bed in the maternity suite we're occupying until the baby is ready to come home.

Wyatt is pressed up against my side, her head on my shoulder, her warmth seeping into me and our daughter sleeping in her arms.

We haven't been able to stop staring at her, our fingertips lightly tracing her ears, her nose, the dark tuft of hair on top of her head. And her smell? Don't even get me fucking started on how good she smells.

"We need to choose a name, Cherry."

"I know." She looks at me with pursed lips. "I know which one I want, what about you?"

"I think we should go with Olivia."

"Yes," she sighs contentedly, running featherlight touches over her cheek. "That's her name. She's Olivia Iris."

I lean down and place a kiss on Wyatt's shoulder.

"Olivia Iris." My hand traces the path of Wyatt's caress. "You were so worth the wait."

THE END.

***

I hope you enjoyed **Breathing Wisteria**! Please consider taking a few minutes to leave a review.

This completes the *Finding Forever* series, but if you would like to find out more about Wyatt's friend

Charlie, you can get your copy of Dating The DILF here!

Keep reading for a sneak peek…

***

Would you like a FREE book? Get your copy of Rule Breaker, a steamy, student/teacher rom com, HERE!

SNEAK PEEK: Dating the DILF by Amali Rose

My eye twitches as an unmistakable aroma fills my office and my nose perks up, ready to hunt down the source with speed and efficiency that would rival a bloodhound. Because what the *actual* fuck.

I'm on my feet before I have a chance to second-guess myself, and when I cross the threshold into my outer office, I have to tamp down a snarl.

"What is that?" I hiss.

Adelaide, my assistant, freezes, her hand halfway to her mouth and her eyes wide. Taking a moment to compose herself, she exhales a quiet breath as though preparing herself to go to battle.

"It goes by many names, Charlie." She furrows her brows, considering me seriously. "Java, Joe, Jitter Juice, Energy Infusion, Rocket Fuel… but I generally refer to it as coffee." She draws the word coffee out slowly, before wrapping both her hands around the paper cup and lifting it to her mouth and taking a long sip.

I bend down, squaring my hands on her desk, and lean forward. The delicious hazelnut scent is practically screaming my name, begging me to come closer. Which I do, much to Adelaide's horror, who is about to topple backward as she attempts to put distance between us.

"I thought we were giving up coffee?" My voice comes out as an annoying whine, and if I was paying attention to anything other than the delicious nectar in her hands, I'd probably hate myself a little for that pathetic display. But my two-day-caffeine-free brain is far too distracted.

"Oh," she startles. "I mean I kind of assumed the *we* part was more rhetorical. I figured my part of the 'we' was more cheerleader-esque. You know, to support *you* to give it up, because..." She pauses to take another sip of her drink, her eyes rolling back in an excessive display of coffee-induced ecstasy that I really don't appreciate. "I don't want to."

I stand upright, silently pondering where I could hide a body. More specifically Adelaide's body. She's pretty small, so it wouldn't need to be a large space. Perhaps in that manky storage cupboard up on the sixteenth floor? Nobody ever uses it. Of course, I do need her for the Thompson meeting at eleven, so taking her out would have to wait until after that...

"Charlie!" Adelaide flips her long blonde hair over her shoulder and glares at me in exasperation. "You're planning my murder again, aren't you?"

"I don't know what you're talking about." Dragging

my eyes away from the coffee in her hand, I pin her with a look of, what I hope is, polite indifference.

"You look constipated, stop that." She smirks at me and I slump down, leaning against her desk and sighing with defeat.

"Can you get me a coffee, please. An Americano with two extra shots."

"I'm sorry, what? I didn't quite catch that." Adelaide turns her head to the side and lifts her ear in my direction. My jaw starts to ache, and I realize I'm clenching my teeth.

"Go and get me a coffee, Addy, before I fire your ass for being literally the worst cheerleader in the whole goddamn world."

I head back to my office with her laughter ringing in my ears and settle myself back behind my desk just as the internal phone line rings.

"Charlotte Reed."

"Charlotte, Mr. Erickson wants you to meet him and Kendall at seven tonight, to go over the Ultra Bond acquisition with them." My boss' no-nonsense assistant brusquely greets me. "Their plane gets in from New York at six and they'll come here directly."

I hold in a groan, knowing there is no way Louis and Kendall will make it here by seven and I have lost any chance I had of getting out of here before nine tonight.

"Of course, Helen. Conference room three?"

Minutes later I am pulling up the Ultra Bond file to make sure everything is ready for tonight, when Adelaide walks in holding a steaming coffee cup and a small bag that promises some kind of pastry deliciousness.

"I got you a cheese danish while I was there." She throws the bag on my desk and hands me the cup before grinning at me. "Tim says hi, by the way."

I ignore her, and the third-degree burns I'm currently inflicting on my throat as I gulp down my coffee.

"I *said*, Tim said hi." Adelaide's usually melodic southern drawl takes on an annoying lilt.

"That's nice." Tim is one of the young—emphasis on young—men who work on the coffee cart that makes the rounds through our offices. He might possibly have a small crush on me, and he really is very sweet, but I haven't been interested in college boys since I was *in* college.

Adelaide flops into the chair opposite my desk while I lean back in my own chair and quirk a questioning brow at her.

"I'm pretty sure you're supposed to be preparing an affidavit for me right now." I tuck a strand of my brown hair back into the ponytail it has come loose from.

"You were the one who interrupted me, but whatever. Just hear me out." I sigh, resignedly, and give her a nod to continue, knowing she won't let this drop until I do. "I know he's young, but he's legal."

I wait for her to go on, but she gives me nothing else.

"That's it?" I snort. "That's your whole spiel?"

"Well, he's also hot, but I thought even you could see that." She shrugs carelessly.

"I don't have time for 'hot,'" I argue.

"Make time for it! Slut it up all cougar-like and get in that boy's boxers. Your vagina will thank you." Addy laughs.

I bite my lip to disguise a smile. "It's not that simple. If I want to make junior partner in the next couple of years, I don't have time for relationships." I move my chair forward, ignoring Adelaide's groan, and begin rifling through the paperwork on my desk. "Which reminds me, Louis and Kendall want to be briefed on the UB acquisition tonight." I hand her a pile of papers. "Can you make me copies of this report before you get back to the affidavit?"

"What time did you get here this morning?"

I blink slowly a couple of times, considering her question. "Six-thirty, why?"

"Six-thirty." She shakes her head and I already know I'm not going to like where this is going. "And after this meeting tonight, you'll get out of here at, what? Nine, nine-thirty?"

"What's your point, Addy?"

"That's a fifteen-hour day. And you're doing that more and more often lately. Not to mention you're here most weekends."

Every weekend, but that seems ill-suited to my argument right now.

"It's the job, you know that as well as I do."

"Do you like the job?" Her question stops me short

and I try to come up with an answer that will pacify her.

"It's a good job. It has great benefits, it's secure and the pay is—"

"Do. You. *Like* it?" She bites her lip and levels me with an exasperated look. "Are you passionate about it? Does it fill you up?"

This right here is why you should never work with your friends.

"I'm passionate about the law," I defend myself.

"You're passionate about negotiating deals so rich assholes can become even richer assholes?" Her voice oozes disbelief.

"I need—"

"You need to get laid." It's said with a roll of her eyes and it's the final straw.

"I need security," I snap. "I need to know that I have the resources to take care of myself and provide for myself. If you have a problem with that, then I'm sorry, but I also don't really care."

"Okay, okay." She holds up her hands in surrender. "I'm sorry, I know this job is important to you. I just want you to remember that it's not the *only* important thing." She stands and smooths down her skirt. "Life can be so much more than what you're making of it, Charlie. Love and relationships don't have to mean you lose something. Sometimes they're the reason you *get* everything."

I watch her walk out, her words hanging heavy in the air, before I turn to my computer and get back to work.

The gentle sunlight is warming my back as I make my way into the huge converted church that is home to my yoga class. The teacher, Dee, began running these classes a few years ago, not long after I started working at Harris & Erickson, and after seeing a leaflet stuck on a coffee shop notice board, I decided to give it a try to see if it helped with my stress levels. I can't say it did much for my stress overall, but I fell in love with the way yoga made me feel. How it made my body stronger and my mind sharper. I've been a devotee ever since and this class is a staple of my Saturday routine.

Yoga is also where I met Adelaide. At the time it seemed like serendipity. After a few classes where we ended up on mats next to each other, sharing our muttered moans of disbelief at some of the positions our goddess-like instructor could get herself into, we went out for a coffee one day. It was there that we discovered a mutual love of coffee and boy bands, as well as the fact that I was looking for a new assistant, while Addy had just completed her paralegal certification.

Kismet.

I find her as soon as I walk into the large room, in the back-right corner, our preferred spot. She's rolled out her mat and is sitting in a seated forward bend, stretching her hamstrings, which I know are sore from a session with her personal trainer a few days ago.

Things were awkward after our words yesterday and I know that was my fault, so sucking in a deep breath I walk over and greet her with a big smile. She eyes me cautiously, but it only takes a moment before a grin slides across her face.

"You're late, I wasn't sure if you were coming." There is no malice in her voice, only curiosity, and I'm grateful she's letting me off the hook and we can move on from yesterday.

I roll out my mat and take a spot on the ground beside her.

"Nanna called right before I was about to leave. Apparently she found a photo of us from a vacation we took to Saugatuck when I was ten, and it was imperative she tell me all about it right that instant." I can't help the giggle that slips past my lips when I remember how excited she sounded while she reminisced.

"You must miss them, how long has it been since they moved? Six months?"

"Yeah, almost that." I grimace as I stretch my own hamstrings, trying to loosen them up before class starts. The burn reminds me that I need to renew my gym membership. One yoga class a week just doesn't cut it. "They love Florida though, so that makes it easier. Every time I talk to them they sound happier than the last."

Adelaide pulls a bottle of water out of her bag and gulps some down, nodding in agreement. "That would definitely help. Still, how old were you when you started living with them? They're practically your parents. I couldn't imagine my parents not living here. Although, sometimes that sounds like a dream," she says wryly.

"I didn't live with them until I was sixteen. Mom left me with them a lot of the time, but I was always going back and forth between them and wherever she was living at the time." The familiar anxiety begins to creep up, remembering those years of tension and arguments. The confusion and dread that weighed me down daily. "When I was sixteen, I'd had enough of it all and I asked Nanna and Poppa if I could move in with them."

"Not gonna lie, your mom sounds like a legit nightmare."

I shrug and consider what she said. "She is who she is. I honestly don't think she wants to be this way, but at this point, I know she'll never change."

Our conversation comes to an end when Dee calls for everyone's attention, directing us to move into child's pose.

"Hey," Adelaide whispers. "Coffee after class?"

I pause, envisioning the pile of work on my desk and knowing I won't get into the office before lunchtime if I go with her.

"Of course," I whisper back.

CHAPTER TWO

MILES

I take a long swig of my beer and try to keep my eyes on the big-screen television that is playing the game above the bar. Despite my best efforts, they keep getting drawn to the table of girls to my left, where a cute blonde has been checking me out for the last ten minutes.

It has been almost a year since my disastrous television experience, which is an awkward amount of time. Too long for every sidelong glance to be a side effect of it, but too short to be able to discount that thought completely.

For all I know, blondie over there might just like what she sees. *Or* she's a rabid dilfie—DILF groupie—which is far more common than you would think, considering how much of an asshole that show portrayed me as.

B.L.—before Lulu—I would have been all over whatever she was offering. I was always on the hunt for *The One*. For my happily ever after. Always chasing what my parents had. After my daughter arrived, I realized I don't have the luxury of messing around with maybes and possibilities anymore.

It was what drew me to the whole shitshow that was *Dating the DILF* in the first place. What a stupid fucking name. I pick up the bottle and take another long pull of my beer, but the bitter rush of regret is all I taste.

A firm slap on my shoulder pulls my head out of my ass and I can't stop the grin when I look up and see my kid brother, Grayson, standing there.

"You have the same shitty expression that my last girlfriend had when I took her cat to the groomers and had them shave it to look like a lion." He pulls out the chair next to me and collapses into it. "She was so pissed, but it was funny as fuck and totally worth the week without sex."

"You're a dick." But I can't help but laugh when I imagine the look on his ex's face. She was a full-blown Kardashian wannabe with a huge stick up her ass and she treated that cat like a child.

The waitress comes over and we order a round of beers, my last for the night.

"Who's winning?" Gray nods toward the television.

"The Bulls are up by five, three minutes left until halftime."

We spend a few minutes catching up while we wait for our drinks to arrive and I have forgotten all about the girl from earlier when I feel a gentle tap on my shoulder and I turn around, only to come face to face with her.

"Hi." Her voice is low and kind of raspy, in an unexpected way. Incongruous to the girl-next-door vibe she gives off. "I'm so sorry to bother you, but my friends and I were talking and, well, are you the guy from that show?" She points to the table next to us. "My friends are convinced you're the guy from that DILF show."

Beside me, Gray covers his mouth to disguise a laugh while I have to swallow down the burn of impatience, the desperate desire to fuck right off and escape her predatory gaze.

But I have no one to blame but myself for this. I let myself get sweet-talked into something with bullshit promises when I should have known better.

So instead, I give her an appraising look and try to decide which camp she falls into. The women who approach me ultimately fall into one of two. The ones who want to rip my dick off and force-feed it to me or the women who want to do much more pleasurable things with it. Not that I would ever give them the chance.

She must mistake my silence for some kind of encouragement, because I feel a light tickle on my arm and, when I look down, I find her fingers trailing along it in a way that is a hell of a lot more intimate than it should be, considering I haven't spoken one word to her yet.

I guess that's my answer.

Remembering all the public relations lessons I got before the show, I slip on a mask of professionalism and give her a bland smile.

"That was me."

"Oh my God!" She squeals and turns to her friends. "It is him!" Turning back to me, she steps closer, her body now pressed up against my thigh. "You know, there's nothing hotter than a guy with a baby. You were so sweet with your little girl in that one episode."

Oh, fuck no.

"Yeah, that wasn't my daughter," I grit out. Making sure Lulu didn't appear on the show was the one *good* decision I made. But I know which episode she's talking about. It was a bogus babysitting setup with Toni? I think that's who it was anyway.

"Oh." She shrugs, her hand sliding lower until it's cupping my dick and she leans in, close enough to whisper suggestively. "Well, I really wanted to fuck you after that episode."

How to go from friendly stranger to inappropriate dilfie in one easy move, ladies and gentlemen.

"Whoa, okay, slow your roll there, beautiful," Grayson quickly interjects while I try to tamp down my annoyance. "I'm going to have to ask you to stop manhandling my brother and step away from the table."

The look on her face is pure shock and I can't help but chuckle as I remove her hand from my dick. "While I appreciate the offer, I'll have to pass."

I watch a myriad of emotions flit over her face before it settles on anger. "Whatever, you were an asshole anyway." And she does what could only be described as flounce back to her table.

"He really is," Gray calls out to her retreating back. "Consider yourself lucky you got away unscathed!"

She flips him the bird.

"I think I'm in love." He clutches his chest and blows her a kiss.

I laugh at his over-the-top theatrics, grateful he is here to diffuse the situation.

"Christ, I think that's the first time a girl's hand on my dick has ever made my balls shrivel up." I gulp down the rest of my beer.

"You're clearly not hanging around the right girls then." He grins over his drink.

"I don't even want to know what that means, fuckface."

"Shit, that reminds me." Gray puts his beer down and pulls his phone out of his pocket. "I saw this on my feed today and it's fucking hilarious. Hold, please." He starts scrolling, his finger is flying across the screen and he's already chuckling to himself. "Here."

He sticks his phone under my nose, and I see an old-fashion-style wanted poster with my face on it. Apparently, I'm wanted for being a "giant douche nozzle and most likely having a small penis." Reward is two hundred and fifty grand.

Huh, I would have thought I would be worth more than that.

I knock the phone out of his hand, and he curses at me as it lands on the table with a loud thud.

"What the fuck, man? That shit is expensive." He snatches it back up and cradles it to his chest while throwing me a wounded look.

Asshole.

"You know." He points at me, waving his finger

almost violently. "You used to have a much better sense of humor about this shit."

"Yeah, well, that was ten months, three million insults, two hundred and seventy-five thousand indecent proposals, one hundred and ninety thousand threats of violence, eighty-two marriage proposals, and twenty-three baby-momma offers ago." I lean back in my chair and shake my head. "Now it doesn't seem so funny."

He eyes me strangely. "That's oddly specific, but I take your point."

"I'm just sick of everyone thinking I'm a cheating little bitch."

"No one who knows you would ever believe that bullshit," he counters.

"It's not the people I know that I have to worry about." I know he's right. I know I shouldn't give a fuck what people think but I went on that goddamn show in the first place because I want to find love, and for a single dad running on fumes ninety percent of the time, the offer of having it hand delivered sounded too good to be true.

That should have told me something right there.

Now, every woman I meet thinks I'm either a complete scumbag, or a quick fuck to tell her friends about.

I scrub a hand across my face and sigh. "Ignore me, I'm just feeling pissy because Harvey has been harassing me about doing a reunion show."

"Seriously?" Gray's brows rise. "Didn't they just

finish a second series? How do they have time for reunion shows."

"I know, and there's another series starting next month too. Apparently the DILF is the gift that just keeps giving," I deadpan.

"Dating the DILF." He snickers. "Stupidest fucking name ever."

"Stupidest fucking *idea* ever."

We tap our bottles and cheers to that.

❧

"I'm home." I throw my keys in the dish by the door, flinching as they hit the ceramic bowl and bring my fingers to my temple to massage gently. It's been a long day and my catch-up with Grayson wasn't nearly as relaxing as I had hoped it would be. All I want to do now is sit down in front of the television and relax.

The tiny footsteps that are flying toward me down the hall and the overexcited shrieking that accompanies them, are telling me that's not going to happen anytime soon.

"Daddyyyy!" A tiny blonde tornado throws herself into my arms and I thank whatever deity is watching over us that I have the foresight to brace myself for her onslaught.

"Hey, kiddo." I bend down and lift her up, inhaling her strawberry scent as she nuzzles into my neck. The stress of today falls away when her little arms tighten around my neck.

"Lulu, get your butt back here and finish your dinner," a gruff voice calls from down the hall.

A small growl vibrates against my neck and I try to contain a laugh. My daughter is not a fan of being told what to do.

"C'mon, what did Gramps make you tonight?"

"Nuggets." Her voice is barely a whisper and it seems that my enthusiastic welcome stole the last of her energy. I walk up the hall to our open-plan kitchen living area and her head rests on my shoulder, one hand gently rubbing her eye and the other wrapped around the back of my neck, twirling a lock of my hair around her finger. It's a quirk she's had since she was a baby and I think at this point I find it just as comforting as she does.

"Hey, Dad." I move through the galley-style kitchen and move straight to the dining table, gently placing Tallulah on her booster seat, not bothering with the straps.

She pushes her dinner plate away, a scowl marring her innocent face. "No. I'm done."

"Tallulah Renee, you've barely touched it. I want one more nugget, a spoonful of potatoes and a piece of broccoli eaten before you can be excused."

I duck my head to hide a grin and make my way to the refrigerator to grab a water. The only person I know who is more stubborn than my daughter is my father and seeing them clash is funny as fuck.

"Goddamn it, Gramps!"

Until it isn't.

Turning, I glare at my dad who is rubbing a hand

over his jaw, his brow furrowed, before I shift toward Tallulah.

"That little outburst has cost you your television time tonight. Now eat your dinner." I narrow my eyes at her, and my strict father act must do the trick because she starts shoveling food in her mouth without arguing.

"Jesus Christ, Dad," I hiss when I'm far enough away that Tallulah won't hear me. "You've got to be more careful around her. I swear to God, I heard her say fuck the other day. Then she just stared at me with this angelic look on her face. You're turning my daughter into a deviant."

Dad folds his arms across his chest and looks me hard in the eye. "You're never going to stop her from hearing the words, Miles. It's up to you to teach her not to repeat them."

I huff out a laugh. "That's easier said than done, Old Man."

He pierces me with a glare, and I decide not to push my luck and change the subject.

"She looks exhausted, what did you guys get up to today?" I round the island bench and take a seat, keeping Tallulah within my sights.

"That kid from number seven came over for a play-date." He groans painfully. "Talk about a deviant, *that* kid has a court date in his future, mark my words. Here." My stomach growls loudly at the sight of the plate of food he slides in front of me. "You look tired too. Bad day?"

I chew my food, happy to have some time to

consider my answer, knowing that Dad will have little to no sympathy for my situation.

"Harvey got a hold of my new number and was calling all day." My throat tightens remembering his smarmy voice and the new promises he was throwing around.

"You were a damn idiot getting involved in all of those shenanigans in the first place. I warned you." He shakes his head, disappointment pulsing off him. "Thomas and I both warned you."

He's got me there. He and my big brother did warn me, and when my life came crashing down ten months ago, they were the first to say I told you so. But they were also the first to step in and help me get control back, which takes the sting away from the continued barbs they throw my way.

"I know, Dad." I imagine my face is as petulant as my almost-three-year-old's was ten minutes ago and I try to school my features into a less hostile version of myself.

"Daddy, I'm tired."

I turn to see Tallulah almost falling asleep at the table. I sigh and push away from the island bench where I was eating.

"I'm going to give Lulu her bath, you're good to let yourself out?"

"Yeah." He begins gathering up the dirty dishes and rinsing them. "Go, I'll see you tomorrow morning."

I move to walk behind him and slap him on the back. "Thanks, Dad. I really do appreciate all your help."

He meets my eye, understanding clear and bright. "I know," he answers brusquely. His eyes turn to his granddaughter and his heavy expression suddenly lightens, a grin spreading across his face. "I think you're needed."

I follow the direction of his look and see Tallulah, fast asleep in her mashed potatoes.

CHAPTER THREE

CHARLOTTE

Adelaide: I swear Thompson has a butt plug permanently shoved up his ass.

Adelaide: I mean have you seen the way he walks?

Adelaide: Like a goddamn penguin!

Adelaide: It's unnatural, Charlie. UNNATURAL!

A tired, but good-natured sigh slips past my lips as I read Addy's response to my earlier message. Pulling my keys out of the ignition, I sink back into my seat and type a quick reply.

Charlie: That may be so, but I believe my question was: did you file the paperwork for his continuance?

Adelaide: Yes, I understand that was your question, but I believe it was pertinent that I shared my

observation before I forgot. Because it was funny as fuck, *Charlotte*

Adelaide: And, yes, I filed the paperwork. <rolls eyes>

Groaning, I shove my phone in my purse and take a moment to shake off the stress of the week.

Ice cream. I need ice cream. A pint of mint choc chip will make everything better. It's the one golden rule of life that has proven to be true over and over.

Ice cream fixes everything.

I climb out of my beloved Prius, ignoring the bite of my waistband and instead concentrate on the mission at hand. My determination is admirable, if I do say so myself.

A light mist of rain has begun to fall, so I hurry through the parking lot to the beckoning fluorescent lights of the supermarket, the familiar tap of my heels on the asphalt comforting me.

Rushing through the automatic sliding doors, I make a sharp right turn and head straight to the freezer section. This week has been a complete nightmare and all I want to do right now is head home and climb into bed with my delicious, sugary treats and a smart-ass devil called *Lucifer*.

Right on cue, I notice how my pants are stretching uncomfortably across my ass with every step I take, reminding me how long it has been since I spent any time on the treadmill. That would probably be a much better plan.

However, all thoughts of the treadmill disappear when I reach the ice cream section and I stare at the promised land. My eyes dart across the rows of creamy goodness looking for my beloved mint choc chip and the noise that escapes my lips when I can't see it could almost be described as a growl.

A deep chuckle to my right grabs my attention and my cheeks are already flaming before I even turn to see who was witness to my small display of emotion.

The burn intensifies when I find myself face to face with one of the most gorgeous men I have ever seen. The first thing I notice is his height. He towers over me, and considering I stand at five foot seven in bare feet, that almost never happens.

Vibrant blue eyes meet mine, full of mischief, and I allow myself a moment to imagine what it would feel like to look into eyes like that every day. The thought startles me and the moment comes to a quick end when he clears his throat and his teeth sink into his full bottom lip in, what I can only assume is, an attempt to fight the smile quirking his full lips.

A fight he is losing.

A wave of fresh embarrassment washes over me and I duck my head in an effort to avoid his gaze.

"Don't you just hate it when they don't have your favorite flavor?" I force a smile and turn to move away, desperate to leave this moment of disappointment and mortification behind, when the deep timbre of his voice stops me.

"Trust me, nobody feels more passionately about ice cream than I do."

I glance up and take in his easy expression. He's running a hand through his slightly unkempt, dark blond hair, a grin stretching across his face. I notice that his hair isn't artfully tousled. You know the kind of messy that guys spend far too long on, in an effort to make it look effortless? Instead, it looks as though he spends his days running his hand through it, with zero care for his appearance. I try not to question why that endears this stranger to me.

"If they don't have my *Cherry Garcia*, I will burn this place to the ground." He leans toward me conspiratorially. "Can I trust you to have my back if shit goes down?"

My answering laugh is loud and unexpected. Somehow this guy has managed to put me at ease and soothe my awkwardness.

"Of course. Who better to have by your side at a time like that than a fellow ice cream annihilator, stranger or not," I reply, my face the picture of earnestness.

"See, now, you get it!" He shakes his head gravely. "Not many people do."

"Well, fortunately there is plenty of *Cherry Garcia* for you." I nod toward a row full—*full!*—of his addiction. "So it looks like Whole Foods will live to see another day. But unless they get in more mint choc chip pretty damn quick, I can't guarantee how long that will stay true."

His smile matches mine and I try to remember when I have felt such an instant connection to a guy before. Have I ever? If I was a different person, I would flirt a little, and maybe ask him out for a drink. That's what a normal twenty-nine-year-old would do on a Friday night, right?

"I'm Miles, by the way." He offers me a large hand. "I figure if we're plotting to take down grocery stores together, we should probably be on a first-name basis."

I stare blankly at his hand for a moment, trying to remember the last time someone shook my hand in any setting other than business. Failing to find one, I slip my much smaller hand into his and smile at the warmth that immediately fills me.

"Charlotte." We stand there, probably looking like idiots, slowly shaking hands, our eyes glued to each other and I am pretty damn sure the dopey smile he is wearing is mirrored on my own face.

That's when it hits me. We're having a moment. A *moment*, moment. Like in my romance novels when the guy and girl meet and BAM! Instant connection that inevitably leads to a happily ever after.

I'm having a goddamn real-life meet cute. Who knew those things ever actually happened? Not me, that's for freaking sure.

His eyes, that have been slowly moving over my face like a gentle caress (because, yes, this moment is *that* swoony), suddenly zero in on something over my shoulder and widen with delighted excitement.

"It looks like today is both of our lucky day." He points behind me, and when I realize what he is showing me, my grin widens. A lone pint of my adored ice cream has been pushed haphazardly in amongst a row of *Strawberry Cheesecake*. As I stare at the tub, I have to fight the urge to show Miles my gratitude with my tongue. Because if I lick it, it's mine, right?

Shaking my head to dislodge the image, a satisfied sigh slips out on an exhale. Ice cream and a hot guy all in one night? Maybe it is my lucky day.

"I could kiss you right now." Turning, I bend down to grab the ice cream, trying to ignore the pounding of my heart that began the instant his eyes heated at my declaration.

Unfortunately, that's when it happens. The unmistakable sound of fabric tearing. I freeze, the moment suspended in time, as I realize the snug fit of my pants across my ass is now feeling pretty damn comfortable.

And breezy. Definitely breezy.

I'm frozen in horror, my eyes squeezed tightly shut, when the humiliation seeps in and I fully grasp the fact that my thong-clad ass is now on full display for Miles to enjoy.

I guess it's safe to say our moment is well and truly over.

Dating the DILF is AVAILABLE NOW!

Stay Connected

Private Facebook Group: https://www.facebook.com/
groups/amalisrisqueromantics
BookBub: https://www.bookbub.com/
authors/amali-rose
BingeBooks: https://bingebooks.com/
author/amali-rose
Facebook: https://www.
facebook.com/authoramalirose
Goodreads: https://www.goodreads.com/author/
show/17064277.Amali_Rose
Instagram: https://www.
instagram.com/authoramalirose
TikTok: https://vm.tiktok.com/ZS3KAon3/

My newsletter is the best way to stay in contact with
me! You'll get first look at titles, covers and release
dates, plus exclusive sneak peeks!
Sign up here: https://tinyurl.com/y6h3hw9s

More by Amali Rose

Finding Forever Series
(Standalone series)

Under the Cherry Blossoms >> Fling to Forever
Romance
Dandelion Dreams >> Enemies to Lovers/Office
Romance
Amongst the Wildflowers >> Friends to Lovers
Romance
Breathing Wisteria >> Second Chance Romance
Finding Forever>> The Complete Series

Greetings From Avondale Series
(Standalone Series)

Mistletoe Mistake >> Brother's Best Friend/Holiday
Romance
Miss Independent >> Billionaire Romance

Standalones:

Dating the DILF >> Single Dad Romantic Comedy

ACKNOWLEDGMENTS

My deepest gratitude to all the bloggers who have read and reviewed any of my books. The time, love and effort you put into supporting the indie community is invaluable and I cannot thank you enough.

To anyone who reads my books - I have always had a deep passion for reading, so I know how the words we read claw their way into our hearts and find a home there. It stuns me every day that there are people who find joy in my words and I thank you from the bottom of my heart.

Kim, thank you for being my person and always making sure I'm okay. Your friendship means the world to me and I hope you never underestimate that.

To the friends who are always there for me: Kerry, Rachel, Karen, Renee, Antonette and the Sassy ladies. I love you!

Annie, you're a ray of sunshine! Thank you for always championing me, you're a wonderful friend!

Kim, Rachel, Tamara & Tre thank you so much for your early feedback on this story. As always, I was pushing right up to the very last minute lol but your enthusiasm for this story motivated me to keep going. I can't thank you enough!

Tijuana Turner, your fresh eyes and perspective helped make Cherry & Irish's story all that it could possibly be and I'm so grateful to you for that. Thank you so very much for taking a chance on me!

My betas: Lauren Harwood, Katrina Haynes, Cassy Kubehl, Heather Packer & Heather Poll, your input was invaluable. Thank you for taking the time to read Wisteria and share your insights with me.

It takes so many people to get one book ready to publish, and I am so lucky to have some incredible people working with me. Huge hugs and mad love to Ellie from My Brother's Editor, Judy from Judy's Proofreading, Ben from Tall Story Designs and the entire team from Give Me Books. Thank you so much for your incredible work. My book baby is better thanks to each and every one of you.

Finally, my ST: Antonette Santillo, Cassy Kubehl, Devon Farrow, Heather Poll, Katrina Haynes, Kristi Smith, Lauren Harwood, Rachel McLean, Tamara

Harrington & Tre Talbot. There aren't enough words
to possibly express how much I appreciate every single
one of you. You're all extraordinary and I love you!

Huge love & hugs!
Amali xox